"Willard, you have possibilities."

—Anonymous

"ANONYMITY LIVES! . . . Espy, the humorist, gifted wordsmith and raconteur (author of AN ALMANAC OF WORDS AT PLAY and OYSTERVILLE), has given Mr. Anonymous a name and a history and has given us, in fact, the kind of man we always knew was behind all that wonderful nonsense and durable wisdom."

The New Orleans Figaro

"Mark Twain at his most playful might have written this story . . . charming fun." *Los Angeles Times*

"MR. ANONYMOUS IS SIMPLE DELIGHTFUL FUN. With great tongue-in-cheek humor, Espy reveals for the first time that those hundreds of poems attributed to 'Anonymous' over the years were really the work of his Uncle Alfred who is always accompanied by his faithful dog, Author Unknown." *The Phoenix Gazette*

"Interwoven with Espy's account of Uncle Allie's long and fascinating career are innumerable samples of his writing; an appendix includes more works of the Anonymous clan. The themes are legion—alcohol, animals, love, philosophy, nonsense, literature. . . . ESPY HAS DONE ALL LOVERS OF LITERATURE A GREAT SERVICE." *Newsday*

The Life and Works of Mr. Anonymous

Willard R. Espy

AVON
PUBLISHERS OF BARD, CAMELOT AND DISCUS BOOKS

AVON BOOKS
A division of
The Hearst Corporation
959 Eighth Avenue
New York, New York 10019

Published by arrangement with Hawthorn Books, Inc.
Library of Congress Catalog Card Number: 76-19765
ISBN: 0-380-45047-x

First Avon Printing, July, 1979

Printed in the U.S.A.

CONTENTS

Part I
THE LIFE AND WORKS OF MR. ANONYMOUS

Part II
SELECTED WORKS OF THE ANONYMOUS CLAN

AUTHOR'S NOTE

The statements about my height and appearance on pages 68 and 103 of this book are lies. So are any and all references to Mr. Anonymous and Author Unknown. The rest of the book is completely factual, including the disappearance of my great-uncle Alfred Richardson in the Klondike in 1879.

A number of verses that some anthologies credit to Anonymous are missing here because other authors have laid claim to them. Frequently attributed to him, for instance, is

> The Centipede was happy quite
> Until a toad in fun
> Said, "Pray, which leg goes after which?"
> That worked her mind to such a pitch,
> She lay distracted in a ditch,
> Considering how to run.

Unfortunately, however, Bartlett's *Familiar Quotations* says Mrs. Edward Craster is author of the conceit, and I must bow to higher authority.

A familiar and delightful humorous verse, attributed by both Carolyn Wells and Ralph A. Lyon to Anon., is

The Modern Hiawatha

> When he killed the Mudjokivis,
> Of the skin he made him mittens,
> Made them with the fur side inside,
> Made them with the skin side outside,
> He, to get the warm side inside
> Put the inside skin side outside;
> He, to get the cold side outside,
> Put the warm side fur side inside.
> That's why he put the fur side inside,
> Why he put the skin side outside,
> Why he turned them inside outside.

❧

But in Arnold Silcock's incomparable "Verse and Worse," he says the takeoff is by George A. Strong.

On page 45 I accept Mr. Anonymous's claim to authorship of a quatrain about cheese-mites, though I have seen it credited to A. Conan Doyle. The verse doesn't sound like Doyle to me, and besides Mr. Anonymous should be given the benefit of the doubt *part* of the time.

If an anonymous favorite of yours is missing in the following pages, it may be because some bloodhound of an anthologist has discovered the real author. If, on the other hand, *you* know who wrote something claimed here by Mr. Anonymous, tell me, so that I can take him down a peg.*

I regret that Edwin and Dale, my surviving brother and sister, play but minor roles in this account. They paid little if any attention to Mr. Anonymous—whose true appellation, indeed, they never learned in his lifetime—or he to them. They sometimes acted as if he weren't even there.

Finally, I can only bow my head in shame if you agree with Mignon Franco, my beloved typist, that I should not have made myself out to be "such a nasty, horrid little boy." I *was* a nasty, horrid little boy.

* Soon after the first printing of this book, I was informed that Christopher Isherwood is responsible for "The common cormorant or shag" (page 148). My apologies to Mr. Isherwood, and shame on Great-Uncle Allie.

INTRODUCTION

The mails are getting slower, but by now some of you may have received your copy of *Punch's Almanac* for 1856, with its eulogy to that prolific writer Anonymous, or Anon. If so, you know why I, the only living man to whom Mr. Anonymous revealed himself in the flesh, have felt it incumbent on me to preserve this record of our life together. Says *Punch*:

> Of Anon but little is known, though his works are excessively numerous. He has dabbled in every thing. Prose and Poetry are alike familiar to his pen. One moment he will be up the highest flights of philosophy, and the next he will be down in some kitchen garden of literature, culling an Enormous Gooseberry, to present it to the columns of some provincial newspaper. His contributions are scattered wherever the English language is read. Open any volume of Miscellanies at any place you will, and you are sure to fall upon some choice little bit signed by 'Anon.' What a mind his must have been! It took in every thing like a pawnbroker's shop. Nothing was too trifling for its grasp. Now he was hanging on to the trunk of an elephant and explaining to you how it was more elastic than a pair of India-rubber braces; and next he would be constructing a suspension bridge with a series of monkey's tails, tying them together as they do pocket-handkerchiefs in the gallery of a theater when they want to fish up a bonnet that has fallen into the pit.
>
> Anon is one of our greatest authors. If all the works that are signed with Anon's name were collected on rows of shelves, he would require a British Museum all to himself. And yet of this great man the world knows so little that it is not even acquainted with his Christian name. There is no certificate of baptism, no moldy tombstone, no musty washing-bill in the world on which we can hook the smallest line of

speculation as to whether it was John or James or Joshua or Tom or Dick or Billy Anon. Shame that a man should write so much and yet be known so little. Oblivion uses its snuffers, sometimes, very unjustly. On second thought, perhaps, it is as well that the works of Anon were not collected together, for it would be found that frequently he had contradicted himself—that in many instances when he had been upholding the Christian white of a question, he had afterward turned round and maintained with equal warmth the pagan black of it. He might often be discovered on both sides of a truth, jumping boldly from the right side over to the wrong and flinging big stones at anyone who dared to assail him in either position. Such double-sidedness would not be pretty, and yet we should be lenient to such inconsistencies. With one who had written so many thousand volumes, who had twirled his thoughts as with a mop on every possible subject, how was it possible to expect anything like consistency? How was it likely that he could recollect every little atom out of the innumerable atoms his pen had heaped up?

Anon ought to have been rich, but he lived in an age when piracy was the fashion and when booksellers walked about, as it were, like Indian chiefs, with the skulls of the authors they had slain around their necks. No wonder, therefore, that we know nothing of the wealth of Anon. Doubtless he died in a garret, like many other kindred spirits, Death being the only score out of the many knocking at his door that he could pay. But to his immortal credit let it be said that he has filled more libraries than the most generous patrons of literature. The volumes that formed the fuel of the Barbarians' bonfire at Alexandria would be but a small bookstall by the side of the octavos, quartos, and duodecimos he has pyramided on our bookshelves. Look through any catalog, and you will find that a large proportion of the works in it have been contributed by Anon. Indeed, the only author who can in the least compete with him in fecundity is Ibid.

A pertinent summary. It requires, however, one correction and one addendum. The correction: Mr. Anonymous was not dead in 1856; the *Punch* eulogy was premature. He, or his avatar, was writing more prolifically than ever, as you can easily confirm by a visit to your library. The addendum: The foregoing *Punch* article is uncredited. It was, of course, written, in one of his whimsical moments, by Mr. Anonymous.

PART I

THE LIFE AND WORKS OF MR. ANONYMOUS

"That finest of English writers, Anon."
—A. H. Buller, F.R.S.,
late professor of botany
at the University of
Manitoba

1

WHEREIN MR. ANONYMOUS IS FIRST CALLED TO MY ATTENTION

Save for an ache in my legs as I climb the stairs to bed, I consider myself in good shape for my sixty-six years, and expect to live many more. I still have time enough to complete the definitive *Encyclopedia Anonymica* which has taken most of my spare time almost from the moment I could first read "Hickory Dickory Dock." Even unfinished, this work already eclipses Halkett's overly touted, seven-volume *Dictionary of Anonymous and Pseudonymous Literature*.

In view of a trove of new material that has just come to me, however, I do not expect the *Anonymica* to appear for at least another quarter century. It therefore seems suitable to present without further delay this preliminary sketch of Mr. Anonymous's life and of our experiences together.

Since the greatness of Mr. Anonymous must be filtered through my own imperfect senses, you would be well advised to bear the nature of that filter in mind as you read.

I entered this sad world at 6.05 A.M. on the eleventh day of December in the year of our Lord 1910. My birthplace was my parents' bedroom in a small frame cottage (since destroyed) in downtown Olympia, capital of the state of Washington. The family had arrived there while I was still homuncular; my father, a native of the sparsely settled southwestern corner of the state, was the choice of the citizens of Pacific and Wahkiakum counties to represent them as state senator, at a stipend, I believe, of five dollars a day.

The Espy family never amounted to much, but always

to something; at least we knew who we were. Mr. Anonymous had our sort in mind when he wrote

> I belong to that highly respectable tribe
> Which is known as the Shabby Genteel
> Too proud to beg, too honest to steal.

The exact instant of my birth is on record because my brother Edwin, then not quite two, the previous evening had stuffed into himself his first wedge of angel-food cake. He then had begged his way into my parents' bed on a plea of bellyache. At 5.03 A.M. he was removed, objecting loudly, to make room for me. One hour and two minutes later, objecting just as loudly, I arrived to replace him.

I was an ethereal-appearing infant, with violet-colored eyes of the giant economy size, set off by long dark lashes; I looked through rather than at my surroundings. "That one," said the hired girl, "is not long for this world." Mama marked the words, and on the erroneous assumption that I had been delivered in a crate marked "fragile—right side up with care," gave me special handling.

In 1913, legislative service being a luxury my father could no longer afford, we returned home to the isolated settlement of Oysterville, where Papa owned a thousand acres of empty oysterbeds and another thousand or so of tide meadows and marshland. On these latter he ran stock and raised hay and vegetables. Oysterville was and is located on Shoalwater Bay (now called Willapa Harbor), near the point of a narrow, tree-covered sandspit thirty miles long, springing from the mouth of the Columbia River. The village, founded in 1854, prospered for half a century on the tasty oysters that crowded the banks of the bay channel. But the oysters died out, and by the time my memory begins there could not have been more than a dozen families still in the neighborhood, cultivating truck gardens and milking cows.

On December 10, 1913, I threw back my tiny shoulders; spread my legs to settle my feet more solidly on the floor; and announced, "Tomorrow I won't be a baby any more; I'll be three years old." This news unaccountably stirred the risibilities of my elder siblings—Medora, 13; Suzita,

11; Mona, 9; and Edwin, almost 5. Helen-Dale, eleven months my junior, could not yet appreciate the hilarity. For the next several days the others would greet me with this singsong:

I'm three years old, and like to wear
A bow ribbon on my hair.
Sometimes it's pink, sometimes it's blue;
I think it's pretty there, don't you?

This was a canard; I wore no ribbon, though my hair could have used one. It was uncut except for bangs, without which I should have been as blind as a sheepdog looks. Until I reached at least my second year of school, older boys frequently grasped this unkempt mop in both hands and rotated me like a sling. I took pride in the attention, and credit the continuing vitality of my hair to that isometric exercising of my hair roots.

The verse irritated me, though, and at one point I accused Medora of having made it up to tease me. She denied the charge, declaring the stanza had been around for years.

"If you didn't write it," I persisted, "then who did?"

"Nobody did," said Medora.

"*Somebody* had to."

"No. It's anonymous."

"What do you mean—anonymous?"

"I told you—nobody wrote it."

"You mean Anonymous is nobody?"

"I mean Anonymous is somebody nobody knows, and little boys should stop asking questions that have no answers."

Yet Anonymous had to be *somebody*. The problem idled in the undercurrents of my mind and surfaced a few mornings later when my father, drawing up his chair for his usual late breakfast of mush, weak coffee, and limp bacon, pointed his Van Dyke beard at my mother, who was seated across from him, and inquired, "Good morning, Helen—have you used Pear's soap?" He was repeating the headline of a popular advertisement of the day. Youngsters frequently taunted each other with the question, holding their noses to make the point clearer.

Obviously, however, my father was referring to quite a different situation. Mama blushed, lowered her heavy-lashed eyes, which drooped at the outer corners, and looked confused.

I asked, "Why do you keep saying silly things like that, Papa?"

Mama answered, doubtless more for his benefit than for mine: "Because men *are* silly, silly."

"Was it silly for someone to write 'Good morning—have you used Pear's soap?' "

"Not exactly; he wrote it to make more people buy Pear's soap."

"But *who* wrote it?"

"The same person," said Papa, "who wrote, 'You press the button—we do the rest.' "

"Eastman Kodak!" we chorussed.

"Or, 'Ninety-nine and forty-four one-hundredths percent pure.' "

"Ivory soap!" we shouted.

"Or, 'The Rock of Gibraltar.' "

"Prudential Life," announced Medora.

"Or, 'Ask the man who owns one.' "

"Packard," we responded in unison, though none of us had ever ridden in or even seen an automobile.

"Or, 'The instrument of the immortals!' "

"Steinway piano!"

"Or, 'Food shot from a gun.' "

"Puffed wheat!" said Suzita. "Puffed rice!" said I.

"Or, 'Time to re-tire.' "

"Fiske!"

"Or, 'The sweetheart of the corn.' "

"Kellogg's!"

"Or, 'The skin you love to touch.' "

"Woodbury's facial soap!"

"Or, 'Ask dad—he knows.' "

"Sweet Caporal cigarettes!"

"Somebody," said Papa, "once wrote

When your client's hopping mad,
Put his picture in the ad.
If he still should prove refractory
Add a picture of his factory."

“But the *companies* didn’t write those slogans,” I said. “Who did?”

“Nobody knows,” said Papa. “Some anonymous writer.”

There leaped into my mind a full-color picture of a dusty, paper-heaped office where an old man named Anonymous sat, scribbling endlessly on foolscap, “Good morning—have you used Pear’s soap?”

Over the following months, I spent most free moments mastering letters of the alphabet, then words, then sentences, working my way through the books that crowded our library shelves and spilled about the chairs, beds, and floors.

As soon as I could put words together, I noted how many passages—particularly the brief poems and stories designed for pre-readers—bore the attribution “Anonymous,” frequently abbreviated to “Anon.” How, I asked myself, could one person write so much?

When my fourth birthday approached, I deliberately selected a poem by Mr. Anonymous to remind my family of the impending anniversary. I recited the verse as we were chatting around the dinner table after dessert—and this time no one laughed:

> My birthday is coming tomorrow,
> And then I’m going to be four;
> And I’m getting so big that already
> I can open the kitchen door;
> I’m very much taller than Baby,
> Though today I am still only three;
> And I’m bigger than Bob-tail the puppy,
> Who used to be bigger than me.

Scarcely a high point in literary annals, one would think; but the recitation aroused as much fluttering and squawking at that table as if a fox had slipped into a chicken coop.

“Who taught you that, Willard?” asked Mama. “I know *I* didn’t.”

“And *I* didn’t,” added Medora.

“Nobody taught me,” I said. “I read it in a book.”

Everyone at the table began to babble (except for Dale, who was still working on her custard dessert, and my father, who looked at me with a little smile lurking between his moustache and his goatee). "Are you pretending you can really read?" . . . "I don't believe" . . . "But when" . . . "Prove it!"

"I will," I said grandly. Pushing back my chair, I marched off for the evidence, and returned with a book. "Here is another one of Mr. Anonymous's verses. And you, Medora"—here I stuck out my tongue—"and you, Suzita"—here I stuck out my tongue again—"won't understand it at all."

"Be polite to your sisters, Willard," said Papa. When Papa spoke, I obeyed. "I'm sorry," I said; "I was only teasing." I read aloud:

I might not, if I could:
  I should not, if I might;
Yet if I should I would,
  And, shoulding, I should quite!

I must not, yet I may;
  I can, and still I must;
But ah! I cannot—nay,
  To must I may not, just!

I shall, although I will,
  But be it understood,
If I may, can, shall—still,
  I might, could, would, or should!

If my earlier recitation brought on a babble, this one produced a stunned silence. The fact that I could really read had been accepted and dismissed; the new question was—and several moments passed before Mama put it—*what had I just read*?

"You all heard the poem," I said, my tone doubtless patronizing. "You can figure it out as well as I can."

"But it didn't seem to mean *anything*," said Mama, looking appealingly at her husband and children as though one of them might be hiding the explanation.

Papa took another sip of his lukewarm coffee. "For a guess, Willard," he said, "didn't that particular verse amuse you precisely *because* the words made no sense?"

"Oh yes, yes," I exclaimed. "How did you know? Mr. Anonymous does that all the time. He did it when he wrote

> When we think a thing, the thing we think is not the thing we think we think, but only the thing we think we think we think.

"He loves to write things just to make people laugh. And some day I'll be able to, too."

"He didn't make *me* laugh," said Medora.

Reading was soon second nature to me; and as my skill improved, my curiosity about Mr. Anonymous increased. Whenever I came across one of his compositions, I marked the place with a piece torn out of a newspaper, in anticipation of the time when I could write well enough to copy the passage into a notebook. These discoveries, though I did not know it at the time, were to become the initial entries in my still-pending *Encyclopedia Anonymica.* Thus, I actually began my lifework when I was little more than four years old.

Two of the first entries came to my attention because of a circumstance of which I was utterly unaware: that my father and mother were deeply in love. They had met at college in California, where Papa was preparing for a career (to be aborted by family adversities) as a teacher of Latin. The adversities had forced him to bring Mama from San Francisco to Oysterville to live out her life among alien corn, in a village where privies hid behind the honeysuckles, and chickens laid eggs under the barns and sheds. Citified to her bones, there was nothing about Oysterville to fill her being except her family and her books. Mama read in every spare instant. Even while she polished the furniture, using a cloth the size of a woman's handkerchief wrapped around her index finger, she held an open book in her other hand, and her eyes were on the book more often than the dusting.

Nevertheless, she considered living in Oysterville a minor price to pay for being with Papa. Without him, she was only half-alive. Once, setting the dinner table, she automatically put the platter of roast pork at his place for carving, forgetting momentarily that he was away for the night on business. As she realized her mistake, her face emptied of blood, and she turned away without a word to carry the platter to her end of the table. Later that evening, while she was sitting with the children around the nursery stove before bedtime, I heard her murmur, more to herself than us:

There's nae luck about the house,
There's nae luck at a'
There's nae luck about the house
When our gudeman's awa'.

The thought instantly flashed through my mind that only Mr. Anonymous could have composed that verse. I asked Mama to write it down for me. It will appear some day in the *Encyclopedia Anonymica*, just under another verse with which Mr. Anonymous himself provided me years later:

Fifty years and three
Together in love lived we;
Angry both at once none ever did us see.
This was the fashion
God taught us, and not fear:—
When one was in a passion
The other could forebear.

Rainy days are not uncommon in Oysterville, the average annual precipitation being a hundred inches. I used the rain to exploit my mother's conviction that I was a fragile package. On wet days she kept me indoors, where I happily galloped my hobby horse—reading—beside the library fireplace or by the nursery stove. I laid down my book of the moment only long enough to take a log from the woodbasket and drop it onto the failing fire. It heightened my sense of well-being to know that Papa and Edwin were floundering in the tempest outside, mending fences, digging potatoes, weeding beets, chasing and milking cows, slaughtering bull calves, feeding chickens and hogs, pitching hay down from the loft, cleaning out manure, and going through all the other chores that were part of life on a farm. Mama might at least have set me to washing dishes or sweeping floors; but she was opposed on principle to boys doing girls' work.

It was her pride and glory that all her children liked to read; but my preoccupation with Anonymous puzzled her. One day she heard me repeating to myself, "The best things, when perverted, become the very worst: So Printing, which in itself is no small Advantage to Mankind, when it is Abus'd may be of most Fatal consequences."

"Why," she asked, "do you want to memorize that particular sentence, Willard? Aren't many lines more beautiful? Why not memorize,

> Silently, one by one, in the infinite meadows of
> heaven,
> Blossomed the lovely stars, the forget-me-nots of
> the angels?"

"Oh, I learned Longfellow long ago," I said impatiently. "But it was Mr. Anonymous who wrote about printing. When I find him I intend to learn exactly *how* he thinks printing might be abused."*

And I had no doubt I would find him. In looking for him, I went through the works of countless known authors. I could not have been more than five, for I had not yet entered school, when I all but drowned in John Stuart Mill's *Principles of Political Economy*. This discomfited Mama; she would have preferred to have me read romantic poets and novelists of the Victorian period. Papa, however, seemed to grasp that I was less interested in Mill's view on a subject of which I knew less than nothing than I was in the clarity with which he expressed himself.

After Mill I took up the Bible. This was no reading sprint; it took me four years to plow my furrow from

* By coincidence, Mr. Anonymous explained this point to me a few weeks before his death, which—again by coincidence—took place on the 500th birthday of Caxton's Press and—still more coincidentally—the hundredth anniversary of the birth of Papa. By 1545, said Mr. Anonymous, New England had a Royal Printer, and by 1557 "printing was restricted to presses authorized by the Crown, with unauthorized books and presses to be destroyed by Wardens of the Stationers' Company."

Genesis through Revelations, even though I skipped much of Leviticus, and all the begats.

But Mr. Anonymous was at the heart of it all. Any conversation, sunset, fragrance, or mood might send one of his phrases flashing across my mind. Even dear old Mrs. Wirt, who lived across the lane, served as his agent. Because our house had the only indoor water system in the village (not so complete as to include toilets; but we did pipe water into the kitchen from barrels on the roof), she often found it easier to tap our faucets than to prime her own pump. Besides, she told us, our water was sweeter than hers. Several times a day she would rap on the living room door, and enter beaming, swinging an empty five-gallon pail and calling, "It's only me, after a bucket of water!" Mrs. Wirt, in her seventies, was rosy and grandmotherly; her interest was less in the water than in the younger Espy children, whom she managed to spoil on each visit. She would gather us into her lap and tell stories or croon songs, virtually all of which turned out to have been the work of my favorite author. We were endlessly enthralled with "A frog he would a-wooing go," "The monkey married the baboon's sister, / Smacked his lips and then he kissed her," and others of that ilk.

Mr. Anonymous even became part of my bedtime ritual, although he was later to deny any responsibility for Papa's standard good night:

Good night
Sleep tight
Don't let the fleas bite
And sweet dreams.

In Oysterville, Mr. Anonymous pointed out, the fleas certainly did bite; my belly in the morning was an archipelago of inflamed, well-scratched bumps. Mr. Anonymous reasoned, therefore, that Papa had made up those lines himself, though they might well have been inspired by that briefest of verses, "Adam / Had 'em," written by an early member of the Anonymous clan. There was no doubt that the clan could claim credit for the prayer repeated nightly, by Edwin, Dale, and me, kneeling by our beds:

Now I lay me down to sleep
I pray the Lord my soul to keep
And if I die before I wake
I pray the Lord my soul to take.

Some Anonymous created the lines that chased each other through my mind on wintry nights, when the coal oil lamp had been blown out, the teeth of the windows were chattering, and the wind swooped and screamed like seabirds outside:

From ghoulies and ghosties and long-leggety beasties
And things that go bump in the night,
Good Lord, deliver us!

Papa was more sympathetic to my search for anonymica than Mama was. She regularly returned to her argument that people with real everyday names had originally written everything, and that "anonymous" simply meant the name had been forgotten or lost. My father, on the other hand, appeared to accept as reasonable my contention that there must be some living Anonymous, descended perhaps from a tribe of them going back to the Romans and Greeks. Papa even sought out anonymous passages for my collection. He quoted their Pidgin English nursery song:

Singee songee sick a pence
  Pockee muchee lye;
Dozen two time blackee bird
  Cookee in e pie.
When him cutee topside
  Birdee bobbery sing;
Himee tinkee nicey dish
  Setee foree King!
Kingee in a talkee loom
  Countee muchee money;
Queeny in e kitchee,
  Chew-chee breadee honey.
Servant galo shakee,
  Hangee washee clothes;
Chop-chop comee blackie bird,
  Nipee off her nose!

He also delighted in "The Naughty Darkey Boy":

There was a cruel darkey boy,
  Who sat upon the shore,
A catching little fishes by
  The dozen and the score.

And as they squirmed and wriggled there,
  He shouted loud with glee,
"You surely cannot want to live,
  You're little-er dan me."

Just then with a malicious leer,
  And a capacious smile,
Before him from the water deep
  There rose a crocodile.

He eyed the little darkey boy,
  Then heaved a blubbering sigh,
And said, "You cannot want to live,
  You're little-er than I."

The fishes squirm and wriggle still,
  Beside that sandy shore,
The cruel little darkey boy
  Was never heard of more.

Papa tossed me high and caught me low to the accompaniment of

Down went McGinty to the bottom of the sea,
All dressed in his best suit of clothes . . .*

* Mr. Anonymous once told me that "McGinty" was one of the few poems he had written in both French and English. The French version:
Monsieur McGinté allait en bas jusqu'au fond du mer,
Ils ne l'ont pas encore trouvé;
Je crois qu'il est certainement mouillé.
Monsieur McGinté, je le repète, allait jusqu'au fond du mer,
Habillé dans sa meilleure costume.

Another of Mr. Anonymous's bilingual poems, "The Little Peach," tells the sad fate of a child who ate an unripe fruit. It begins in French:

At the bottom of each toss we would shout the name of the author in unison: "A N O N Y M O U S!"

One morning, as he pitched manure through the windows of the horse stall, Papa announced to me between grunts,

I know two things about the horse,
And one of them is rather coarse.

"Anonymous!" I shouted.

"Anonymous," he agreed. "Your Mr. Anonymous belongs to a versatile family, Willard. One of them wrote one of the most famous poems in English." He recited it, resuming his pitching at the same time, so that the lines sounded like this:

Une petite pêche dans un orchard fleurit,
Attendez à mon narration triste!
Une petite pêche verdante fleurit.
Grâce à chaleur de soleil, à moisture de miste.
Il fleurit, il fleurit,
Attendez à mon narration triste! . . .

I don't have the English version of "The Little Peach" around, but the general idea of the starting lines is something like this:

A little peach from an orchard root
(Ah! listen to this sad tale!)
First blossom, then bloom, then finally fruit!
With thanks to the sun, and the rain to boot
The little peach grew to a tempting fruit
(Ah! listen to this sad tale!) . . .

Mr. Anonymous once wrote, in similar vein:

Verdancy

A green little boy in a green little way
A little green apple devoured one day;
And the little green grasses now tenderly wave
O'er the little green apple boy's green little grave.

Sumer is icumen in (*scrape*! *pitch*!)
Lhudde sing cuccu! (*scrape*! *pitch*!)
Groweth sed, and bloweth med, (*scrape*! *pitch*!)
And springeth the wude nu. (*scrape*! *pitch*!)

I preferred the couplet about the horse.

2

WHEREIN MY GREAT-UNCLE ALLIE PAYS AN UNEXPECTED CALL

The spring brought occasional splendid days, when the sun poured out its heart as riotously as a false lover swearing to be faithful forever. The sky was at one moment silver as a looking glass, at another blue as a jay. White clouds flew in irregular protean ranks overhead, their shapes changing from camels, into dragons, into birds, into hook-nosed old women. The air was murmurous with a subliminal roaring of breakers, striking the ocean beach a mile to the west.

One unusually warm Sunday in my sixth year, after the worshipers had straggled out of the Baptist church across the street, I returned home, picked up a book, and sat down to read. In a few moments, however, my attention was distracted by a transitory lightening of the windows in the library; the sun was finding a way through the clouds. It occurred to me that I might read outside by sunlight, a pleasure dear to me to this day. So without bothering to inform my mother, I left the house and settled myself in the sandpile Papa had dug for us children between the northwest corner of our yard and the sand ruts that constituted the main street of Oysterville. I lay prone, my book open before me. My elbows were propped in the sand; my chin was in my fists.

Though I have no idea what I was reading, I know exactly what I was wearing, because it was the same costume I wore every Sunday: a homemade variant of a small boy's sailor suit, set off at the shoulders by a wide white collar and fastened at the throat by white laces. The blouse, of a checkered material, covered the top of identically checkered pants, which descended halfway to the knee. My footgear consisted of socks and sandals, both white.

It was hard in those days to distract me from my reading. (A family joke is that when our house once caught on fire, the men dashing back and forth with buckets of water had to jump over me, because I was lying in the midst of the bedlam reading comic supplements.) Nonetheless, I gradually became aware of a cawing of crows to the south. The sound grew louder, as if the crows were coming my way; I first suspected, and then was certain, that their caws were either accompanying or trying to drown out a human voice raised in song. Though the tune was familiar, at first I could not distinguish the words. At last I identified a refrain familiar to anyone who had ever sung around an Oysterville piano:

As I was a-walking one morning for pleasure,
  I spied a cow-puncher all riding along;
His hat was throwed back and his spurs was a-jingling,
  And he approached me, a-singing this song:

Whoopee ti yi yo, git along, little dogies,
  It's your misfortune, and none of my own.
Whoopee ti yi yo, git along, little dogies,
  For you know Wyoming will be your new home.

An instrumental accompaniment underlay the song, and each stanza concluded with a mournful howl that could not have emanated from a human throat. I lifted my gaze from the book and watched a turn in the road, a thousand feet away, to see what would appear. First, low over the trees, the crows came flying; then a stranger, accompanied by an enormous dog, strolled into view. I stood up to see better.

The arrival of a stranger would have been startling in any event, for to all intents and purposes strangers had vanished from Oysterville. Perhaps they had been wiped out two generations back as a by-blow of the measles and smallpox that had exterminated our Indians. But these two visitors would have staggered anyone merely by their looks.

Both the man and dog were of extraordinary size. The

man must have stood close to six and a half feet tall, nor could he have weighed less than two hundred and fifty pounds; yet some parts of his body were scarcely more filled out, from all appearance, than my own. As he drew nearer, I could see that his features were sharply etched and his face even thin; yet the dewlap beneath his chin swung like a bull's. A woman eight months pregnant could scarcely have boasted so great a belly; its circumference, I learned later, came to sixty-three inches. His head was shaped like an oversized gourd standing on its stem end, but a gourd that had undergone much crossbreeding; before that moment, I had no idea how apt the expressions "cauliflower ears" and "rutabaga nose" could be. He wore a derby hat; steel-rimmed, thick-lensed glasses magnified his eyes.

His thinner parts were as unprecedented. His neck—long, with a large Adam's apple—appeared too fragile to bear the weight of his head, which as far as I could see maintained its place through a balancing act; the head was in constant delicate motion, adjusting to the movements of his body as tightrope walkers adjust to the swaying of their ropes.

His neck was set into shoulders too narrow for so enormous a man. His heavy white sweater, of the knitted, patterned variety we now call Irish, could not hide the meagerness of his upper torso, or the spindling of his arms. His legs looked like a pair of asparagus stalks that had forgotten to stop growing.

As he sang, he plucked at a mandolin slung from a rope around his neck. Another sling held a box camera at the apogee of his belly. Strapped to his shoulders was the biggest valise I had ever seen—a sort of steamer trunk with a handle. Atop the valise was a wooden contraption of a kind that I could not immediately decipher. He advanced with an incongruous lightness of foot—a ponderous glide, reminiscent of the progress of a great cat.

More striking than the man, if possible, was the dog, which stood as high as a newborn calf. It had short, yellowish hair, exposing every prominence and hollow of its grotesque body. Out of kindness, I would like to euphemize the appearance of the creature, as I have done for its owner, by using metaphorical terms; but unfortunately its every repulsive detail was unmistakably labelled Dog. The face was in size as that of a wolf-hound, but squashed in a fashion reminiscent of a horribly magnified Pekinese. If the least attractive physical characteristic of every canine species could be enlarged to impossible proportions, and then fitted together like a jigsaw puzzle, such a monstrosity as this would be the result.

I was so abrim with curiosity that no room was left for self-consciousness. I stared unblinking; the two stared back. When they were about fifteen feet away they came to a halt. The man deliberately laid down his mandolin (I remember how oddly long the handle seemed), shrugged his valise from his shoulders, and unstrapped from it the wooden contraption I have mentioned—a three-legged stand. He adjusted the legs of the stand carefully in the sand, then set his camera on top, opened it like an accordion, and concealed the camera and his head under a black cloth. The dog meanwhile seated himself—I shall no longer refer to him as "it," for no animal could have been more egregiously male—and unrolled a tongue that hung from his mouth like a dripping red carpet.

From under the black cloth came a high, muffled voice. "Brush off that sand, boy," said the stranger. "Fine, fine—just so—just so." The camera clicked. He removed the black cloth and refastened the camera to his belly.

The crows continued to wheel and caw. I could see the big brown eyes behind the man's glasses. They seemed to swim about like paired sea creatures; I could imagine pressing my face against those glasses as one might against a fish tank for a better view of the mysteries inside. Above them, his lashes and brows were auburn, as was the unkempt hair that grew over his ears and shoulders.

I do not know how long our mutual scrutiny lasted. At last he said in a voice so high that it seemed almost a falsetto, "Have you forgotten your manners, young man?" (When I quote him hereafter, please remember the pitch of that voice. Remember also that except when he was singing, he always broke off each syllable as if it were a separate word, identical in length and emphasis with all the rest: "Have – you – for – got – ten – your – man – ners – young – man?")

"Oh, excuse me," I said. "Good morning, sir. You see I am not used to strangers. Especially strangers taking pictures of me."

"Then permit me to introduce myself. I am Alfred Bennett Richardson. My friend here is Author Unknown."

It was easy to see how the dog got his name. No canine sire, except possibly Cerberus, would admit to such a get as this; and Cerberus had to be counted out, since it stands to reason that as a three-headed dog, he would have produced a three-headed son.

"How do you do, Mr. Richardson," I said. My answer did not satisfy him. He scowled at me, and the short yellow hair on the dog's shoulders bristled.

I said, "Oh—and how do *you* do, Author Unknown."

"Arf!" said the dog.

But his master still seemed discontent. He said, slowly and distinctly, as if I might be deaf,

> I am rather tall and stately,
> And I care not very greatly
> What you say or what you do.
> I'm Mackail—and who are you?

"But you said your name was Richardson."

For a moment he pressed his lips together so hard that I could no longer see them. Then he said, "My boy, you do not *look* stupid. I am hinting, boy, *hinting*. Let me try again":

> My name is George Nathaniel Curzon,
> I am a most superior person.

"*Now* do you understand?"

"Well, not exactly," I said. "You said first your name was Richardson, and then Mackail, and now Curzon—"

"*Curzon*?" he exclaimed with indignation.

> I am the great Professor Jowitt
> What there is to know, I know it.

I am the master of Balliol College,
And what I don't know isn't knowledge.

With that he suddenly snapped his fingers and leaped into the air, wattles and belly swaying. The heels of his heavy shoes cracked together before he hit the ground again. He continued to jump in the same way for as long as it took him to sing,

Is that Mr. Reilly, can anyone tell?
Is that Mr. Reilly that owns the hotel?
Well, if that's Mr. Reilly, they speak of so highly,
Upon me soul, Reilly, you're doing quite well.

"And now," I continued, "you claim to be somebody named Reilly—"

"Oh, my great-grandmother's ghost, boy! Haven't you got it through that tangled thatch of yours that I am trying to induce you to do me the honor of telling me *your* name?"

"Well, then, why didn't you ask?" I replied indignantly. "You must have known my name was not Mackail, or Curzon, or Reilly. It is Espy."

Mr. Richardson clapped a hand dramatically to his forehead. "I knew it! I knew it!" he exclaimed. "From the moment I saw you sitting like a frog in that sandpile, I said to myself, 'He has to be one of Harry and Helen Espy's boys!' "

"I am, yes sir."

"Of course—of course! The spit and image of your mother's father! And would this be your parents' home?" He had been folding his tripod as he spoke, and he now sighted along it at our house. The part nearest to hand—a one-story woodshed, kitchen, and dining room—the street. A living room (formerly the laundry), connected this area to the older main house, a two-story, clapboard affair that showed signs of having once been painted white with green trim. Scalloped trim dripped from the second-story eaves, and the windows scowled under heavy green eyebrows.

"Yes, sir," I said, "that is where we live."

"And the board fence—would that be to prevent the likes of me, from peering into the yard?"

"Oh, no, sir. It's to keep stray cattle from breaking in."

"And the windmill?"

A silly question. The windmill, located beside the covered porch that ran alongside the dining room and living room to the front door, was obviously there to pump water into the barrels on the roof. My politeness was wearing thin. "To make the wind blow, I suppose," I said, and scuffed a sandal sullenly in the sand. He cocked his head at me, more quizzically than in irritation. I even thought the folds of his face gathered together into a smile.

"Ah, a saucy one you are, lad," he said. "Well, I suppose I was saucy at your age, too. The important thing is that you are Helen's son. I'm sure she's a fine mother, boy?"

"Indeed she is," I said proudly, and added, "Yes, and a hard-working one, too."

"Ah yes. I am sure she takes care in scrubbing the pantry shelves?"

"Why, certainly she does."

"Alas for the microbes then," said Mr. Richardson:

> Two microbes sat on a pantry shelf
> And watched, with expressions pained,
> The milkmaid's stunts;
> And both said at once,
> Our relations are going to be strained.

I said, "Papa says she works too hard."

"No doubt—no doubt. I once wrote an epitaph for a woman who worked too hard. Would you like to hear it, boy?"

"My mother needs no epitaph," I said, feeling peevish. "I would like you to call me by my right name, though."

"But how can I, when you have not told me what it is?"

That was true enough. I said, finally remembering my manners, "I'm sorry. My name is Willard. My friends call me Wede. And of course I would like to hear you recite the epitaph, if you wish."

“I appreciate your interest, Willard. I call the song, ‘On a Tired Housewife:’ ”

Here lies a poor woman who was always tired,
She lived in a house where help wasn’t hired;
Her last words on earth were: ‘Dear friends, I am going
To where there’s no cooking, or washing, or sewing.
For everything there is exact to my wishes,
For where they don’t eat there’s no washing of dishes.
I’ll be where loud anthems will always be ringing,
But having no voice I’ll be quit of the singing.
Don’t mourn for me now, don’t mourn for me never.
I am going to do nothing for ever and ever.’

I said, “Did you really write that?”

“Indeed I did, my boy—I mean Willard. Indeed I did.”

“I like it very much,” I said. “Would you teach it to me?”

He smiled full out for the first time, and I saw that his teeth were white and even. Either they were false, or he was not as old as I had thought. “A very bright boy you are, Willard. I should have known. Now the fact is that I have come to call on your parents—”

“Papa isn’t here. He and Edwin are mending fence at the Douglas donation land claim.”

“That is quite all right,” said Mr. Richardson. “At this moment I am interested in meeting your mother.”

“Oh dear!” I said. “I’m terribly sorry, but it upsets Mama when guests arrive without warning. Right now she is blacking the kitchen stove, and you see—”

“Not another word. Not another word. You just run in and tell your mother that her Uncle Allie is outside, back from the dead so to speak, and that she is to stop blacking her stove. She is to clean herself up, and put on her prettiest dress. When she is quite ready to receive me and Author Unknown, come out and tell us. Meanwhile we shall wait here in perfect contentment.”

As it turned out, he was indeed Mama’s Uncle Allie. My great-grandfather, Horace Richardson, had two sons; the elder, my grandfather Daniel, was born in Massachusetts in 1851, and the younger, Alfred Bennett, in California in 1860. In 1879, when Alfred was nineteen and his niece, my mother, eleven, Alfred left San Francisco to make his fortune in Yukon gold. His family had not seen or heard of him since.*

I carried out his instructions. My mother left the half-blacked stove, bathed herself in a laundry tub (which with Medora's help she filled halfway to the top, using alternate buckets of hot and cold water), put on a clean dress, and did something to her hair. She then invited my great-uncle into the house. Shortly afterward Papa and Edwin returned home, and for the rest of the afternoon Uncle Allie filled us in on his life since 1879. It appeared that he had been washed overboard one stormy night off the Alaskan coast, fortunately less than half a mile from land. Despite the money belt he was wearing, he had managed to swim ashore before the icy waters congealed him. He reached the beach near the cabin of three English trappers, who took him in, removed his clothes, rubbed his icy flesh until it was scarcely less red than the fire that glowed through the sides of their roaring stove, helped him into long johns, and wrapped him in a blanket. When they considered him sufficiently thawed, they bedded him down in one of their bunks.

The trapping season was over. When his hosts set off for Montreal a few days later to sell their furs, Uncle Allie accompanied them. From Montreal, the quartet took ship for England. Allie spent awhile in London, and then in Edinburgh, where he enrolled in the university and earned a first in literature. He studied thereafter at the Sorbonne in Paris, at Tübingen in Germany, and at the University of Madrid in Spain. Shortly before 1900, he reversed field completely. He returned to the States, and spent several years in the western cow country before becoming an instructor in French at Columbia College.

* In *Oysterville*, a recent family reminiscence, I said that "Allie grew up sickly; the one remaining picture of him as an adolescent is reminiscent of the 'Sorrows of Werther.' In 1879, not yet nineteen, he joined an expedition to the Arctic. He never returned."

The picture to which I referred appears in this book. But my statement was wrong; for if the Allie reminiscent of the 'Sorrows of Werther' never returned, certainly the gross caricature that was Uncle Allie did.

In an entirely different part of New York he claimed to have operated a clothing establishment called the Fat Man's Store.

When Mama asked why he had not communicated with his family, he shrugged, exchanging a glance with Author Unknown.

Mama was too overwhelmed by her resurrected uncle to push that question harder (Papa never pried into personal matters; he was reluctant to embarrass anyone). Besides, her attention was distracted by Author Unknown. Mama was not sentimental about pets. We had a collie dog that could take the board fence at a bound. We had the usual cats with their usual kindles. In addition, I owned a Scotch terrier named Jack. (This was because one of my mother's fixed myths about me was that I loved all dumb creatures; I once managed a whole luxurious afternoon of reading in bed as a result of rushing into the house, weeping because I had found a dead sparrow outside.) Except for Jack, ours were working pets; the cats killed mice, moles, and snakes; the collie herded cows; and all lived outside the house. To have a creature the size of an average calf sitting in her living room, shifting his bulbous gaze from one human being to another as if he followed the conversation, disturbed Mama to such an extent that she was never able to recall more than snatches of what Uncle Allie told us that day.

At dinner, Author Unknown placidly seated himself by his master. The dog did not use a chair, to be sure, but he was so huge that, sitting on the floor, he could lean his swollen head on the tablecloth. And he did.

Papa's benediction was unusually long, even for him. By reason of Uncle Allie's miraculous reappearance, Papa felt compelled to call down blessings on the English, the Scots, the Irish, the French, the Germans, and indeed the citizenry of every nation in which Uncle Allie had reported spending a night. While the benediction was going on, Uncle Allie proceeded to remove a flask from his hip pocket, fill his water glass nearly to the brim with a dark and strong-smelling liquid, and sip from it, nodding between sips at each particularly eloquent turn of my father's invocation.

Papa was a man of inflexible principles. When the

prayer was over, he said, "Allie, I am very sorry, but Helen and I agreed before our marriage that alcoholic beverages were never to be drunk in our home."

Uncle Allie nodded. "Quite right, too," he said, taking another sip. "Company might misunderstand. It's a fortunate thing for me that I'm one of the family. Dinner wouldn't be dinner for me without my schnapps."

For a moment Papa was tongue-tied. Uncle Allie went on: "My family has had a saying about alcohol for six hundred years. It goes, 'Alcohol sloweth age, it strengtheneth youth, it helpeth digestion, it abandoneth melancholie, it relisheth the heart, it lighteneth the mind, it quickeneth the spirits, it keepeth and preserveth the head from whirling, the eyes from dazzling, the tongue from lisping, the mouth from snaffling, the teeth from chattering, and the throat from rattling; it keepeth the stomach from wambling, the heart from swelling, the hands from shivering, the sinews from shrinking, the veins from crumbling, the bones from aching, and the marrow from soaking.' "

"Why—why—I never heard of such a saying!" said Mama. "Daddy is no prude, but he has never drunk anything stronger than milk in his life. I remember we had Mr. Samuel Clemens to dinner one evening, and even Mr. Clemens was served milk! Oh—and coffee, of course."

"And did Sam drink the milk?" asked Uncle Allie with interest.

"I believe so," said Mama. "I do remember that he had to leave early for some reason—"

"Don't misunderstand me," said Uncle Allie, pouring the remainder of the liquid carefully from his flask into the glass. "Our Richardson forebears"—here he paused a moment to pick his words—"spiritual forebears, that is, were always moderate in their habits. One of them wrote the 1820 manifesto of the Massachusetts temperance society, and you can't be much more moderate than *that.*"

"Was it Grandpa Horace's father?" asked Mama. "David, I mean?"

"No, he wasn't the one, but he was close kin. I'll recite the manifesto to you, Helen; you really must memorize it. Tomorrow I'll write it down. It goes this way:

" 'We, the undersigned, recognizing the evils of drunkenness and resolved to check its alarming increase, with consequent poverty, misery, and crime among our people, hereby solemnly pledge ourselves that we will not get drunk more than four times a year, viz., Fourth of July, Muster Day, Christmas Day, and Sheep-Shearing.'"

Papa said hastily, "Well, we'll discuss it later, after the children are in bed. Come now—down with the oysters."

I should perhaps explain that at this time in the life of the Espys we ate by the whim of nature. When Papa slaughtered a calf for the market, he sold the liver if the price for liver was good; otherwise we ate the liver ourselves. As a last resort, we could fall back on oysters. Tonight was an oyster night. The meal began with oyster cocktails and continued through oyster soup and fried oysters. We may have had sugared oysters for dessert. None of this bothered Uncle Allie, who, as I was to learn later, would eat anything and as much of it as was put before him. It did cause him, however, to recite, beating time with his fork, a passage by Charles Dickens—the only time in my life I ever heard him quote a named author:

"Dando, the oyster eater," quoted Uncle Allie, "used to go into oyster shops, without a farthing of money, and stand at the counter eating natives, until the man who opened them grew pale, cast down his knife, staggered backward, and struck his white forehead with his open hand, and said, 'You are Dando!!!' He had been known to eat twenty dozen at one sitting. . . . He was taken ill, got worse and worse, and at last began knocking violent double knocks at Death's door. The doctor stood beside his bed, with his finger on his pulse. 'He is going,' says the doctor. 'I see it in his eye. There is only one thing that would keep life in him for another hour, and that is —oysters.' They were immediately brought. Dando swallowed eight, and feebly took a ninth. He held it in his mouth and looked round the bed strangely. 'Not a bad one, is it?' says the doctor. The patient shook his head, rubbed his trembling hand upon his stomach, bolted the oyster, and fell back—dead. They . . . paved his grave with oyster shells."

"And a good way to go," said Papa. "Ah—I notice the

dog's place has not been set. I'm sure that Helen would be glad to bring another plate."

"Never mind, never mind," said Uncle Allie. "I fed Author Unknown earlier. He is perfectly happy just sitting here, sharing the benefits of a most stimulating conversation."

3

WHEREIN THE IDENTITY OF MR. ANONYMOUS IS REVEALED

Uncle Allie's announced plan was to remain with us a few days and then hike south to Oakland for a get-together with his older brother Dan. He generally traveled afoot, he said, to keep his figure. (Despite visual evidence to the contrary, he considered himself an enviable physical specimen. And in view of his Falstaffian build he was at least remarkably agile. I have seen him stand on a block of wood six inches high and touch the palms of his hands to the ground without bending his knees.)

But the weeks blurred by, and he did not leave. Instead, summer being now well rooted and the weather fair, he spent most of his days—Author Unknown at his side and me straggling behind—in a systematic exploration of the area around the village.

Each expedition was a major event. Uncle Allie first prepared for himself, Author Unknown, and me a picnic luncheon on which a regiment could have subsisted. The usual components included sandwiches of rat cheese between thick slices of bread; one thermos bottle (he called it a Dewar bottle) of coffee and milk mixed half and half, and another of whiskey (un-iced); fried chicken; potato salad; various meats for the dog; and milk for me in a tightly stoppered lard can. (I later learned that Uncle Allie was a bit of a gourmet and had once written verse recipes for *Punch.*) Mama kept an ample supply of cold cuts and such in the pantry for him. She was not, however, permitted to participate in his picnic preparations, or even to enter the kitchen while they were going on, though she occasionally fluttered at the door.

Once our lunch was stowed away in his knapsack, he

would arrange his mandolin, camera, and associated gear about his person much as I had first seen them, and we would start out. The crows seemed to know whenever Uncle Allie was aprowl; they followed us, cawing among themselves as if our activities were an in-joke that only crows could appreciate.

Uncle Allie was childishly curious about anything connected with nature. Each exploration was unpredictable. We might, for instance, visit the mudflats beyond the bay bank at low tide, wearing hip-length gum boots. Offshore we overturned loose hummocks of grass-covered clay to uncover colonies of tiny, scuttling crabs, each brightly dressed in an individual color. Some were smaller than my thumbnail; some were as big as Uncle Allie's.

Clams, jarred by our footsteps, squirted water a foot into the air. We excavated them from the mud with our hands, careful to avoid the cutting edges of their shells, and sang in chorus:

I am
  A Clam!
Come learn of me
Unclouded peace and calm content,
  Serene, supreme tranquility,
Where thoughtless dreams and dreamless thoughts
  are blent.

When the salt tide is rising to the flood
  In billows blue my placid pulp I lave;
And when it ebbs I slumber in the mud,
  Content alike with ooze or crystal wave.

I do not shudder when in the chowder stewed
  Nor when the Coney Islander engulfs me raw.
When in the church soup's dreary solitude
  Alone I wander, do I shudder? Naw!

If jarring tempests beat upon my bed,
  Or summer peace there be
I do not care: as I have said
  All's one to me;
    A Clam
    I am.

As we wandered farther from shore, the mud was replaced by hard rippled sand laced with shallow sloughs. At the approach to the channel, more than a mile out, the sand dipped beneath water where emerald-green seaweed grew. We groped in the shallows for barnacled clusters of oysters, broke the families into their individual entities with the tap of a hammer, and carried them home in gunnysacks that dripped over our shoulders.

If Uncle Allie's fancy was for the upland, we would strike across the hay meadows, leaving a swathe of bent yellow stalks behind us. Angling westward, we would surmount a ridge, the spine of the peninsula. It was burdened with small bushes of huckleberry and salmonberry, and larger ones of prickly blackberry and gorse. Above a gorse bush, one day, bees were swarming. Uncle Allie informed me that whenever I saw such a sight I must say aloud fast:

A swarm of bees in May
Is worth a load of hay;
A swarm of bees in June
Is worth a silver spoon;
A swarm of bees in July
Is not worth a fly.

We would descend the west side of the ridge into a swamp, where we jumped from tussock to tussock (Uncle Allie more lightly than I), and traverse gloomy groves of spruce and alders. Sometimes we waded across Lehman's Lake (seldom more than a foot deep), continued through the western woods, and clambered to the top of the steep dune that was the inner boundary of the ocean beach. Below us stretched a quarter-mile of bone-white, undulating sand. It was cluttered with bleached roots; logs; stove-in dinghies; and skeletons of fish ranging in size from herring to whales. The surf continued so far into the ocean that only a fingernail-paring of blue water separated it from the horizon. Once in a while we descended to the water line and poked about in the half-buried hulk of the *Solano*, a lumber schooner that had washed ashore the year before I was born.

I habitually carried one book or another, into which I frequently dipped when I would have been better off drinking in my surroundings. Hot with walking, I would drop to the ground and catch my breath. It was an accepted part of our routine that Uncle Allie and I would then take turns reciting verses, always loudly, as if we were shouting into the wind. A frequent choice of my uncle's, pronounced with what I took to be a deliberately exaggerated Scots burr, was

Says Tweed to Tell—
  'What gars ye rin sae still?'
Says Twill to Tweed—
  'Though I ran slaw,
For ae man that ye droon
  I droon twa.'

Or he might proclaim:

The cheese-mites asked how the cheese got there,
  And warmly debated the matter;
The orthodox said it came from the air,
  And the heretics said from the platter.

At times I teased him about his girth—teasing which I must say he took in excellent part. I quoted such lines as

A sleeper from the Amazon
Put nighties of his gra'mazon.
  The reason? That
  He was too fat
To get his own pajamas on.

More frequently, though, our subjects were animals, perhaps because Uncle Allie had made me acutely conscious that however deserted the countryside might seem at a glance, it seethed behind the scenes with insects, birds, reptiles, and mammals: rabbits, skunks, deer, beaver, bear.

Uncle Allie's contributions to these recitals were not

always in the best of taste. One of them nagged at my thinking for years before I grasped its purport:

The rabbit has a charming face;
Its private life is a disgrace.
I really dare not name to you
The awful things that rabbits do;
Things that your paper never prints—
You only mention them in hints.
They have such lost, degraded souls
No wonder they inhabit holes;
When such depravity is found
It can only live underground.

But our verses had one thing in common: They were all the works of Anonymous. Uncle Allie had joined in this hobby of mine even more enthusiastically than my father. He insisted that I memorize one authorless verse after another. "They need friends," he would say; "they are orphans of the storm."

Though all this was more than fifty years ago, I sometimes still wake in the morning, looking forward to a tramp with Uncle Allie. Can it have been less recently than Wednesday last that we basked on the top of the huckleberry ridge, while he focussed his camera on the flooding tide? Is that field of ripe oats still there, cut in two by the road that connects Oysterville with Nahcotta, four miles to the south? Surely it must be—and beyond it the meadow of salt hay, set against Shoalwater Bay. Is the bay full to the brim, sparkling blue against the mainland hills on the other side? Or is it dry as far as the eye can follow?

All the verses we recited will ultimately be available in my *Anonymica*. But even if I had never begun writing them down, they would remain printed in my memory. Silly verses, most of them, like this one:

I have a copper penny and another copper penny;
  Well, then, of course, I have two copper pence;
I have a cousin Jenny and another cousin Jenny
  Well, pray then, do I have two cousin Jence?

❧§❧

Or:

'Tis sweet to roam when morning's light
  Resounds across the deep;
And the crystal song of the woodbine bright
  Hushes the rocks to sleep.
And the blood-red moon in the blaze of noon
  Is bathed in a crumbling dew;
And the wolf rings out with a glittering shout,
  To-whit, to-whit, to-whoo!

Or:

What a wonderful bird the frog are—
When he stand he sit almost;
When he hop, he fly almost.
He ain't got no sense hardly;
He ain't got no tail hardly either.
When he sit, he sit on what he ain't got almost.

Most ubiquitous of all Oysterville denizens were the garter snakes. In the village proper they were mostly little lively fellows, each with two or three bright red, yellow, or green stripes running parallel down its black back. In the marshes they grew larger. We frequently found them sunning themselves in obscene clusters, lying on rotting boards that once had been the walls or floors of cabins. We were walking around such a cluster one day, keeping a respectful distance, when Uncle Allie paused and said, "Would you like to hear a verse I wrote once to a snake?"

Each time Uncle Allie asked me to listen to one of his own verses I felt the same premonitory clutch inside me that I had felt on the day of our first meeting. Somehow, he was connected with the Mr. Anonymous of my dreams. Yet obviously, being my mother's uncle, my own great-uncle, he could not himself be Mr. Anonymous. A living Mr. Anonymous was about as likely to turn up as, say, a living Big Foot, whose huge prints frequently appear in the northwestern wilderness; or the Abominable Snow Man who inhabits the snowy Himalayas. The reality of the Loch Ness Monster and the Great Sea Serpent remained in doubt, though thousands of reliable witnesses had sighted and even photographed them. No one had claimed the barest sighting of Mr. Anonymous.

Uncle Allie commenced in his high staccato scream:

> Prodiggus reptile! long and skaly kuss!
> You are the dadrattedest biggest thing I ever
> Seed that cud ty itself into a double bo-
> Not, and cum all strate again in a
> Minnit or so, without winkin or seemin
> To experience any particular pane
> In the diafram.
>
> Stoopemjust inseck! marvelous annimile!
> You are no doubt seven thousand yeres
> Old, and hev a considerable of a
> Family sneekin round thru the tall
> Grass in Africa, a eetin up little greezy
> Piggers, and wishin they was biggir.
>
> I wonder how big yu was when yu
> Was a inphant about 2 fete long. I
> Expec you was a purty good size, and
> Lived on phrogs, and lizzerds, and polly-
> Wogs and sutch things.

By this time I was clapping my hands and laughing. My giggles approached hysteria as he continued:

> You are havin' a nice time now, ennyhow—
> Don't have nothing to do but lay off
> And ete kats and rabbits, and stic
> Out your tung and twist yur tale.
> I wunder if yu ever swollered a man
> Without takin oph his butes. If there was
> Brass buttins on his kote, I spose
>
> Yu had ter swaller a lot of buttin-
> Wholes, and a shu-hammer to nock
> The soals oph of the boots and drive in
> The tax, so that they wouldn't kut yure
> Inside. I wunder if vittles taste
> Good all the way down. I expec so—
> At least, fur 6 or 7 fete.

You are so mighty long, I shud thynk
If your tale was cold, yure hed
Woodent no it till the next day,
But it's hard tu tell; snaix is snaix.

"Oh, Uncle Allie," I said, "I think it's *terribly* funny."

He looked complacent. "It really has to be seen to be appreciated," he said. "You know—the spelling of the words—a certain aura of—shall we say—illiteracy—?"

I swallowed, clenched my fists with the effort of utterance, and forced out:

"Is that verse in print somewhere, Uncle Allie?"

It was the right question. He smiled and nodded, the flesh of his vast cheeks rising tidally until his eyes were nearly hidden. His wattles flapped and slowed to a stop, like a swing when the old cat dies.

I felt dizzy. I must not move, I told myself; else a shock would shoot through me, as when static electricity jumps. One might expect to feel such tension when a necromancer, having chalked his pentagon on the floor, mutters the phrases designed to summon up the devil. I made myself say calmly:

"Then your name must be signed to the verse."

"In a manner of speaking, yes."

"And to other verses besides?"

"You could say that."

"But Uncle Allie, I have been going through books of verse nearly every day for more than two years now, and I have never found your name."

"The luck of the draw, my boy, just the luck of the draw." But I knew he shared my sense of an imminent confrontation.

"Uncle Allie," I said suddenly, "do you know who wrote, 'Good morning—have you used Pear's soap?' "

He hesitated, as one might before diving into cold water. Then he said, "Why yes, of course I know, Willard. Yes. *I* wrote it."

(*Smoke was rising from the pentagon . . .*)

"And did you sign yourself Alfred Richardson?"

"Of course not. A man doesn't sign an ad, you know."

"But the snake verse—did you sign *that* one Alfred

Richardson?" I was far from motionless now; indeed, I was almost jumping up and down with excitement.

"No, I didn't."

"Why not?"

"Well, Willard," said Uncle Allie, his high voice slow and serious, "the fact is I was—you might say—" he was uncharacteristically groping for words—"I was adopted into a tribe."

"An Indian tribe?"

"No, no—nothing like that. 'Tribe' is not really the right word, either. An old man had a feeling he was going to die—this is hard to explain, I'm sorry—he left me a mission—and his name."

Now I *was* jumping up and down. "The name—the name—what was it?"

"You already know what it was."

"*Anonymous*!" I exclaimed. "*Anonymous*! You *are* Mr. Anonymous!"

"Yes, so I am—for the time being. But you must promise not to tell. Not your father. Not your mother. Not your brother and sisters. Nobody—for as long as I live."

"I promise—I promise! Oh, *dear* Uncle Allie. Oh, *dear* Mr. Anonymous!" I ran and squeezed him the best I could; my head pressed against the lower slope of his belly; my arms barely reached his buttocks. He picked me up and hugged me; I found that I was crying, and that Author Unknown was licking my face.

Next day Uncle Allie announced that it was time to break off his visit. I am not sure all the family was sorry. I had obviously been his pet among the children, which could not have pleased the others. Nor could Mama have regretted losing Author Unknown, though she and the dog had reached a mutually respectful arrangement: she tolerated his presence in the house as long as he stayed as far from her as the space of a room permitted.

As for me, the tears would not stay back. I stood up quietly so as to leave the room before anyone noticed. But Papa, who often seemed to know my thoughts, looked at me and gave his head a tiny shake, as if to say, "Wait." Then he addressed Mr. Anonymous: "Of course we don't want to hold you here, Alfred. I know you are anxious to see Dan,* and I know he is anxious to see you. After all, Dan is getting along in years. But I do hope you will be coming back soon."

"Probably not for a while, Harry. The fact is a little Baptist college down in Southern California has asked me to run their foreign language department, and I find myself tempted."

"I am afraid that knocks out my idea," said Papa regretfully. "I was hoping you might be able to lend me a hand."

"I'd do anything for you I could," said Uncle Allie. "Afraid I'm not much of a farmer, though."

"No, this has nothing to do with farming. I run the local school board, and one of our teachers won't be coming back next year. I had been thinking that if you had no other commitments, you might be willing to take her place."

"Why, Harry, that's a gracious gesture. I'm touched. I really am." Uncle Allie drew a red, wrinkled kerchief the size of a small tablecloth from his hip pocket and proceeded to blow his rutabaga nose.

"We have two schoolrooms, in different buildings—one room for grades one through four, and the other for grades five through eight. It's one through four I'm talking about."

I exclaimed, "Oh, please, Uncle Allie! I'll be starting school, and you can teach me—"

"Harry, would you be willing to trust an old reprobate like me with your own children?"

"Nothing could please me more," said Papa. "I'm afraid you'd have only Edwin and Willard to torment you, though; Dale is not ready for school yet, Mona will be in the sixth grade, and Medora and Suzita go to boarding schools."

"I'm tempted," said Uncle Allie. "I can't remember having a better time than this past month. Willard and I have come to be great friends, and I don't know a place in the world that appeals to me more than Oysterville."

"You haven't seen the rainy season yet," said Mama.

"But I can't accept. You both have been very kind to

* His brother, Dan, my grandfather.

us old hulks"—here he scratched Author Unknown's head —"but we can't impose on you any longer. Helen was working herself to the bone with only her own family to handle. We make two too many. It's time to be going."

Papa held up his hand, palm out. "That part is all taken care of. The Winslow cottage belongs to me, and it's empty. We have some extra sticks of furniture we could install there; the roof's tight; and I think you could bach there quite comfortably."

Author Unknown, who had been stretched out on the hearth, got slowly to his feet, hind end first. He walked over and laid his head in Uncle Allie's lap. For a long moment they looked into each other's eyes.

"If you really mean that, Harry," my uncle said finally, "all I can say is thank you. Give us—that is, give me the night to think the whole matter over, and we'll—I'll—give you an answer in the morning."

I let out the breath I had been holding. There was no doubt in my mind that he would say yes. And he did. To be sure, he left in a few days to visit my grandfather; but he returned to settle into his new home a week before school opened.

4

WHEREIN MR. ANONYMOUS TEACHES SCHOOL

Mr. Anonymous and Author Unknown arrived the second time not as before, unheralded and afoot, but riding grandly beside Henry Lehman on the high front seat of his freight and mail stage. Five days a week a mule and a horse pulled this springless wagon along the sandy ruts between Oysterville and Nahcotta, terminus of the narrow-gauge peninsula railway. The stage carried packages, parcels, persons, or even pups. (Here gargantuan Author Unknown counts as a pup.)

The back of the wagon overflowed with crates and cardboard boxes, containing, apparently, the whole of Mr. Anonymous's possessions. These consisted primarily of books, manuscripts, and correspondence, in such quantities that we had to make room for some of the boxes in our own attic. It took him several days to unpack, and by the time he was settled, school had begun.

I occasionally tramped with him and Author Unknown on weekends, and he dined once a month or so at our house: but he spent most of his non-teaching hours in his cottage. Passersby heard his typewriter firing sporadic staccato bursts. Sometimes they also reported hearing from the cottage, in the small hours of the morning, ribald songs accompanied by the howling of a dog.

How happy I was that first year of school! In December I reached the magical age of six, which I knew then and know now to be the optimum age for a human being. At six I had all the knowledge required to get along in life: I could tie my shoelaces in a double knot; I could identify the local flora and fauna, or most of them, by their Latin classifications, with a little help from my father and Mr. Anonymous; on a clear night I could point out the major constellations. I was aware, moreover, that this was but a fleeting phase of life, to be savored while it lasted. Once I reached seven I would be impatient to become eight; at eight I would want to be nine; and so I would proceed from frustration to frustration until, at some time in the vague future, my world would reverse itself, and my most intense, most hopeless desire would be to start growing younger again.

Besides, I was the possessor of a unique secret and two extraordinary friends. Whenever Uncle Allie looked at me from behind his desk, or Author Unknown from the spot he regularly occupied beside the pot-bellied wood stove, I knew that the three of us were bound together in a mystical trinity, invisible and unavailable to the outside world.

First grade presented one minor problem: outdoor games—hide-and-go-seek, one-old-cat, run-sheep-run, and so on—did not interest me of themselves, nor could I hold my own in them. The most gently tossed softball dropped between my outreached hands. I threw like a girl. I could not make a flat rock skip on water. Though I did not wear glasses—there were no required eye examinations in those days—I was myopic and astigmatic; I never saw the moon walk the night sky without its ghost.

Nonetheless, I enjoyed the companionship of my schoolmates and think they enjoyed mine. They had their bats and balls; I had my books; both sides were satisfied with the arrangement.

The primary grades were taught in a room perhaps thirty feet square, part of an abandoned store building a few hundred feet from my home. I was an early arrival on opening day, even ahead of Edwin—an unusual accomplishment for me, for I was and am still a slow mover.

Joy Christie, a year older than I, was the only child ahead of me in the school yard that morning. He was bouncing a rubber ball against the gnarled trunk of a walnut tree. Joy wore trousers; suspenders with one strap unbuckled; and no shirt. He was barefoot. I was in brown coveralls, buttoned up the front, and wore shoes. His black eyebrows joined over his nose; later, in my adolescence, I remember plucking out any hair that sprouted between my eyebrows, fearing it might be the first span in a bridge to join my brows in an unbroken line like his.

❧

Joy and I had known each other since infancy. Still, custom demanded that as a second-grader he subject me to mild hazing. This he proceeded to do by pointing his right forefinger at me, stroking his left forefinger across it in an immemorial gesture of shame, and chanting,

I saw your hinee
cha cha cha
It's bright and shinee
cha cha cha
If you don't hide it
cha cha cha
I'm gonna bide it
cha cha cha.

I wondered how Joy would react if I told him he was quoting his new teacher.

Perhaps a dozen other children, ranging in age from five to eleven, gradually joined us in the yard. I can still conjure up most of them—Frances and Alice Sargant, neither of whom wore shoes winter or summer; Kenneth Walkowsky, son of an Indian mother and an immigrant Pole; Ed Andrews and his younger brother Mert; a boy who farted whenever he stood up to recite, so that Mr. Anonymous had to keep the windows open even in the chilliest weather; Cyril Curl, whose face was long, like a horse's; Helen Goulter, who wore her auburn hair in curls down her back; Edwin, blond, laughing, the only child besides myself who regularly wore shoes.

Alice Sargant retains a special place in my heart because she and I held a wrestling match on the second day of school; I proposed to her as she held me with both shoulders pressed to the ground. My second proposal, two or three years later, was to Lucille Wachsmuth, and resulted in an engagement lasting at least one or two hours. She was milking a cow, her forehead pressed against its flanks; that moment, when I think of it still evokes Mr. Anonymous's lines in my memory:

When Molly smiles beneath her cow,
I feel my heart—I can't tell how.

❧

That first day, as on every school day thereafter, Uncle Allie rang the school bell at nine o'clock. He sat at a desk; we faced him, seated in two ranks, divided by an aisle. With a few exceptions, the boys sat on the left-hand side of the aisle and the girls on the right. The first grade was nearest the teacher, the next grade just behind, and so on back. An American flag, flanked by steel engravings of George Washington and Woodrow Wilson, was nailed to the wall behind Uncle Allie.

The pupils would read aloud or do their sums on the blackboard one at a time. Discipline under Uncle Allie was not harsh; whispering was endemic, and spitballs and paper airplanes fought frequent battles over our heads. When a fourth-grade boy flung a blackboard eraser that left a white mark on Uncle Allie's cheek, though, my uncle's *savoir faire* deserted him; he lifted the culprit into the air by the back of the neck and laid two mighty swats on the boy's posterior. There was no more throwing of erasers.

That first day I stayed inside at recess, basking in my companionship with my uncle and the dog. No one spoke; Mr. Anonymous and I read, and Author Unknown dozed. Our secret connection was acknowledged only once, when we heard the children outside singing

> Like a leaf or a feather,
> In the windy, windy weather,
> We will whirl around,
> And twirl around
> And all sink down together.

Uncle Allie and I both knew where that song came from. For an instant a smile glimmered between us.

Arithmetic was the only subject I found unkind. When Uncle Allie reproached me one day for looking out the window while he explained sums on the blackboard, I replied snappishly:

> Multiplication is vexation,
> Division is as bad;
> The rule of three doth puzzle me,
> And fractions drive me mad.

He was not annoyed; this was a game we frequently played, to the bewilderment of the other pupils. They accepted without apparent resentment that I was teacher's pet. Yet on matters of discipline he gave me no preference; the palm of my hand still tingles when I think how he would slap it with his ferule for some remark he considered out of bounds. Now, he only inquired mildly,

"Don't you like *any* kind of arithmetic?"

"Not the kind you do with figures."

"What kind, then?"

"This is the kind I like." I drew a deep breath, and piped:

> It was the busy hour of four
> When from the city hardware store
> Emerged a gentleman, who bore
> One hoe,
> One spade,
> One wheelbarrow.
>
> From there our hero promptly went
> Into a seed establishment,
> And for these things his money spent:
> One peck of bulbs,
> One job-lot shrubs,
> One quart assorted seeds.
>
> He has a garden under way,
> And if he's fairly lucky, say,
> He'll have about the end of May
> One squash vine,
> One egg plant,
> One radish.

Uncle Allie scowled, and I scowled back. "Willard," he demanded, "can you give me the definition of a moron?"

"You taught it to me yourself, sir," I replied. (And indeed he had, having written it.) "Morons are 'Those whose mental development is above that of an imbecile (seven years) but does not exceed that of a normal child of twelve years.' "

"Perhaps you should consider your qualifications," Uncle Allie said, and went on, pointing a stern finger at me:

❧

See the happy moron,
He doesn't give a damn,
I wish I were a moron,
My God! perhaps I am!

The children giggled, and my face probably turned red, but such interchanges between me and Mr. Anonymous never upset either of us. No, I am wrong—there was one, only one, that enraged me. He insisted one day that in answering a question I had committed the cardinal sin of saying "I seen." I knew I had said "I've seen." The charge was so heinous, and his refusal to accept my denial so intolerable, that I gathered up my textbooks, marched out the front door, and went home. There I remained, despite all my mother's protestations—my father was away, or the result might have been different—until Uncle Allie came over that evening and formally apologized.

"I have no doubt, Willard," he said, "that you really said 'I've seen,' not 'I seen'; but, my boy, I have concluded that sometimes you need putting down a little, even when you are right."

"Uncle Allie," said I, "or Uncle Anonymous, if you wish, you once created an expression for the mate of a whaler to use on his ill-humored captain. Let me quote it back to you:

" 'All I want of you is a little see-vility, and that of the commonest goddamnedest kind.' "

That ended the nearest thing to a quarrel that I ever had with Mr. Anonymous. For a moment I was left with a feeling of disorientation about our relationship—as if, ever so briefly, Uncle Allie had shown himself more dependent on me than I on him.

But he had a point; I was a bumptious little boy. Often I corrected my schoolmates in the midst of their reciting. Once I climbed the ladder to the attic over the schoolroom and spent half an hour fumbling through the litter there. At length I located some Guffey readers, which I brought down the ladder while one of the boys was doing his sums aloud. In my excitement at my find, I silenced him as a man might silence a barking dog. "Stop!" I shouted. "Listen to this, all of you!" And I read:

In Adam's fall
We sinnèd all.

"Who wrote that?" I demanded. There was no answer, and I went on, "*Anonymous* did, that's who did—and he wrote these too:

Young Obadias,
David, Josias,—
All were pious . . .

Xerxes did die,
And so must I . . .

Zaccheus he
Did climb the tree
Our Lord to see.

All at once I had a cold sensation, as if a gun barrel were boring into my back. I looked around. Author Unknown had risen. His lips were drawn back from his teeth; the short yellow hair on his back was erect, and the expression in his bulging eyes would have frightened Hercules himself. Suddenly I was aware that, however unintentionally, I was treading on the edges of our secret. I said hurriedly, "Gee, I'm sorry. I really am. Excuse me. I guess I just got carried away." And I slunk to my seat.

Uncle Allie prodded and poked me through grades 1 and 2 in my first year, and through grades 3 and 4 in my second. This put me in Edwin's grade, and I was not yet eight when he and I were removed from the primary school to the grammar school, presided over by Mrs. Brooks. It is not the fault of Mrs. Brooks that I remember very little about her except her passion for the poem *Hiawatha*, which she made every pupil learn from beginning to end. With all due respect to Mr. Longfellow, there is a certain sameness to *Hiawatha* that leads on to either torpor or a flurry of spitballs. One afternoon after the waves of Gitchie-Gummee had beaten about me for more than an hour, I raised my hand and when called upon substituted a parody:

This is the metre Columbian. The soft-flowing trochees and dactyls,
Blended with fragments spondaic, and here and there an iambus,
Syllables often sixteen, or more or less, as it happens,
Difficult always to scan, and depending greatly on accent,
Being a close imitation, in English, of Latin hexameters—
Fluent in sound and avoiding the stiffness of blank verse,
Having the grandeur and flow of America's mountains and rivers,
Such as no bard could achieve in a mean little island like England;
Oft, at the end of a line, the sentence dividing abruptly,
Breaks, and in accents mellifluous, follows the thoughts of the author.

"Willard," said Mrs. Brooks, "I think perhaps you read too much and exercise too little. I will write a note to your parents to that effect. And I shall expect you to be ready tomorrow to give us a serious verse."

"Any particular subject, ma'am?" I asked.

"Any subject that interests you."

"Would animals be all right? My mothers says I am very fond of animals."

"Yes, of course. As long as the verse is serious."

The next day, when my turn came, I recited dreamily,

I wish I were a
Elephantiaphus
And could pick off the coconuts with my nose.
But, oh! I am not,
(Alas! I cannot be)
An Elephanti-
Elephantiaphus.
But I'm a cockroach
And I'm a water-bug,
I can crawl around and hide behind the sink.

I wish I were a
Rhinoscereeacus
And could wear an ivory toothpick in my nose.
But, oh! I am not,
(Alas! I cannot be)
A Rhinoscori-
Rhinoscereeacus.
But I'm a beetle
And I'm a pumpkin-bug,
I can buzz and bang my head against the wall.

I wish I were a
Hippopopotamus
And could swim the Tigris and the broad Ganges.
But, oh! I am not,
(Alas! I cannot be)
A hippopo-
Hippopopotamus.
But I'm a grasshopper
And I'm a katydid,
I can play the fiddle with my left hind-leg.

I wish I were a
Levileviathan
And had seven hundred knuckles in my spine.
But, oh! I am not,
(Alas! I cannot be)
A Levi-ikey-
A Levi-ikey-mo.
But I'm a firefly
And I'm a lightning-bug,
I can light cheroots and gaspers with my tail.

The verse trailed off. With my eyes cast modestly down, I made for my seat. Mrs. Brooks said, "Willard! You will apologize at once. You will apologize to me. You will apologize to your schoolmates."

"*Apologize*?" I gasped. "Why do you want me to apologize, Mrs. Brooks?"

"You are making fun of me. You are making fun of all of us."

I heard her with the utmost astonishment. Uncle Allie's high-pitched voice seemed to buzz in my ear:

“*I* would not have thought you were making fun of me or the class, Willard. I would have thought we were all having fun together.”

Suddenly I was an alien, desolate. I raised two fingers in the universal sign that meant, “There is no time to waste; nature is calling—seriously.” When the teacher reluctantly nodded, I went out to the privy, sat on the seat awaiting me, and wept bitterly for a vanished dream.

I refused to apologize, and was sent home. That evening I told Mr. Anonymous about the incident. He hee-hawed like a donkey.

“One of my finest efforts, my boy,” he said, trying to puff out his chest and succeeding in puffing out his belly.

I was recalled to school next day, and Mrs. Brooks made no further reference to my taste in poetry. But neither did she ever ask me to recite a poem again.

Mr. Anonymous stayed at Oysterville for one more school year, to make sure my younger sister Dale received a proper grounding in reading and writing, if not arithmetic. Then he accepted the teaching post that was still waiting for him down South at the University of Redlands.

For the next few years I heard from him but seldom. Anonymous poems, clipped from newspapers or magazines, arrived from time to time, often without an accompanying note. The other day I found one, received not long after the end of World War I:

The Dying Aviator

A handsome young airman lay dying	
(CHORUS)	
	lay dying,
And as on the aer'drome he lay,	he lay,
To the mechanics who round him	
came sighing,	came sighing,
These last dying words he did say;	he did say;
“Take the cylinder out of my kidneys,”	“of his kidneys,”
“The connecting rod out of my brain,”	“of his brain,”
“The cam box from under my	
backbone,”	“his backbone,”
“And assemble the engine again.”	“again.”

"When the court of enquiry
assembles," — "assembles,"
"Please tell the reason I died," — "he died,"
"Was because I forgot twice iota" — "twice iota"
"Was the minimum angle of glide." — "of glide."

At ten, I was still considered frail by my parents, or at least by my mother; if my father thought differently, he did not say so aloud. They were both pleased when any interest drew me from the house and my books into the open air. With Uncle Allie gone, I no longer had an incentive to wander about the fields and marshes; so when my father discovered one day that I had sunk a coffee can into the yard and was knocking the inner core of a baseball into it with a club I had hacked from a tree, he decided to turn me into a golfer. He and the hired man mowed the field back of the house, converting it into the approximation of a nine-hole links; the greens were the areas where the hay was cut a little shorter. Papa ordered a set of golf clubs from Sears Roebuck, and came home from Portland one day with a gallon bucket of beaten-up golf balls. For several months thereafter I concentrated on golf as I had concentrated earlier on books. News of this development provided Uncle Allie with a flood of comic inspiration. My next postcard from him read:

I was playing golf that day
When the Germans landed.
All our soldiers ran away,
All our ships were stranded.
Such were my surprise and shame
They almost put me off my game.

Historians say that Mr. Anonymous was jibing not at me but at Arthur Balfour, First Lord of the Admiralty in the early years of World War I. Perhaps; but certainly his second postcard was directed solely at me:

Lives of golfers oft remind us
How to make our lives sublime,
And departing leave behind us
Divots on the links of time.

A few days later I received a poem which he called the "Old Hundred." It was obviously modelled on Tennyson's "Charge of the Light Brigade":

Half a stroke, half a stroke,
Half a stroke onward,
Into the yawning ditch
Plump! goes a foozled pitch—
This is the scoring which
  Runs up the hundred.
Bunkers to right of them,
Bunkers to left of them,
Bunkers in front of them,
  Showed how they blundered.

Though our exchanges were infrequent, Mr. Anonymous did not dim in my memory. Seven years passed, however, before I saw him face to face again.

5

WHEREIN MR. ANONYMOUS RETURNS

Edwin and I completed grades 4 through 8 in two years, he at twelve and I at ten. Papa then located a teacher qualified to give secondary as well as primary education, who ran us through our freshman and sophomore studies in a single year at the Oysterville school. Thereafter, however, we had to travel by bus each day to the high school at Ilwaco, fifteen miles away. We took the next two grades one a year, and received our high school diplomas when I was fourteen and Ed sixteen. Mama and Papa thought us still a bit young to matriculate at college. We therefore dawdled away another year on a so-called commercial course, covering such skills as typing, shorthand, and commercial arithmetic. Except for the typing, I lost these skills as fast as I acquired them. Unfortunately, from my first day at Ilwaco High School I lost also whatever drive toward intellectual excellence I might have brought with me from Oysterville. Latin and French were typical of the way I treated my courses: I took home the grammar books the first day of school, read them over the weekend, and coasted through the rest of the year on what I could remember or pretend to know.

But it was not Ilwaco that caused this deterioration. It was the onset of pubescence. At twelve, my highest ambition was no longer to write immortal verse but to attain a level of physical coordination that would permit me to put an arm around a girl while steering a car with one hand.

In my junior year I made my third proposal of marriage, this time to the daughter of the driver of the school bus. She was at least three years older than I, and to my intense humiliation she not only laughed but spread the word of my infatuation among our schoolmates.

❧

A year later, I first kissed a girl. (This was also the occasion of my first attendance at a dancing party.) Papa had let Ed and me take the family Ford, Ed at the wheel, and the kiss took place as we were returning our dates to their homes. Mine, Mary by name, was a lovely tow-head. We sat in the dark back seat fumbling for chocolates from a candy box and at intervals fumbling for each other (or perhaps I was the only fumbler). How, I asked myself, did one request a kiss? Or was a kiss something to request? If we talked at all while I brooded on this subject, the conversation was irrelevant to anything in my mind, or no doubt in hers; it must have run along the lines of Bashful Ned's:

"How's your father?" came the whisper,
  Bashful Ned the silence breaking;
"Oh, he's nicely," Annie murmured,
  Smilingly the question taking.

Conversation flagged a moment,
  Hopeless Ned essayed another,
"Annie, I—I," then a coughing,
  And the question, "How's your mother?"

"Mother? Oh, she's doing finely!"
  Fleeting fast was all forbearance
When in low despairing accents,
  Came the climax, "How's your parents?"

This would never do. Had not some sophisticated acquaintance said that all girls melted at whispered songs of love? I cast frantically through my mind for a verse to fit the occasion. Mr. Anonymous murmured inside my head. I said, "Ah, Mary—have you ever heard the saying,

Be happy while y'er leevin,
For y'er a lang time deid"?

"Why, no," she said—I could hear her hand groping for another candy—"what does it mean?"

"It means—it means—oh, look, Mary, do you understand Scottish?"

❧

"Mom came from Finland and Pop from Norway, but I can try."

"Well, somebody wrote a Scottish poem that goes:

Some say kissin's ae sin,
  But I say, not at a';
For it's been in the warld
  Ever sin' there were twa.

If it werena lawfu',
  Lawyers wadna' 'low it;
If it werena holy,
  Meenisters wadna' dae it;

If it werena modest,
  Maidens wadna' taste it;
If it werena plenty,
  Poor folk couldna' hae it."

"Are you saying you want to kiss me?" she asked kindly. "Then—why don't you?"

With the words she turned slightly toward me; I could feel her gum-perfumed breath against my cheek. I could also feel my heart beating.

If Mr. Anonymous had been around, he could have explained to me that kissing requires a certain accommodation of the two heads involved; but he was not. I put my hands over her ears, pulled her to me, and kissed straight on. I am not sure whether our lips touched, but our noses struck with such force that mine began to bleed, while she gasped, "Hey!" Whether after so hard a blow on so sensitive an area she would have gone on to instruct me in the accepted techniques of kissing I was never to learn, for I had no thought now except for my nosebleed. Here was a humiliation that must at all costs be concealed from the world. In a panicky effort to disguise the disaster, I seized a handful of chocolate creams and smeared them around my mouth. I am glad I could not see myself when we dropped Mary at her home. What with one thing and another, she never went out with me again.

All in all, there was little in common between the interests that had preoccupied me when Uncle Allie left

Oysterville in 1919 and those on my mind when he made his return visit in the summer of 1926.

In view of his reputation as a phrasemaker, it may seem a letdown that his first words when he descended from Mr. Lehman's stage (now a Reo truck) were: "My! How you've grown!" Still, it was a natural thing to say. I had shot up until at the age of fifteen I was almost as tall as Uncle Allie himself; my height so embarrassed me that I walked with a self-conscious stoop.

After the usual family greetings, he and I wandered about the farmyard, considering the new horses and cows and yarning about the ones that had died; seeing how some trees had grown, while others had blown down. We leaned against the picket gate of the chicken yard, and Uncle Allie repeated lines I had first heard from his lips as a small boy:

I sometimes think I'd rather crow
And be a rooster than to roost
And be a crow. But I dunno.

A rooster, he can roost also,
Which don't seem fair when crows can't crow.
Which may help some. Still I dunno.

Crows should be glad of one thing, though;
Nobody thinks of eating crow,
While roosters they are good enough
For anyone unless they're tough.

There are lots of tough old roosters, though,
And anyway a crow can't crow.
So mebby roosters stand more show.
It looks that way. But I dunno.

But Uncle Allie had not come north after a seven-year absence simply to reminisce. For some time he had been urging Mama and Papa by mail to send Edwin and me to the college in California where he was teaching languages. He was determined now to settle the matter once and for all, and that evening mustered his arguments one by one. First, Redlands was Baptist; though Uncle Allie entertained no particular creed, he respected the fact that my father was a devout member of the Baptist faith. (Mama was more of an Episcopalian.) Second, the whole family could settle next to the campus during the school term, so that Edwin and I could live at home. Third, the college was small; with only five hundred students, we could count on personal attention for the problems of social adjustment we were bound to experience as underage freshmen. Finally, Uncle Allie himself would be there to guide our steps in the paths of righteousness.

We were taking our places at the dinner table as he raised this last point, and he had the grace to look sheepish when I caught his eye. I credited Mr. Anonymous with many virtues, but few, paradoxically, in what is usually referred to as the area of morals. He cleared his throat, glared at me, and proceeded to drink the tot of whiskey with which he customarily washed down Papa's benediction. Once this benediction was finished, he poured himself another tot from his flask, pushed himself to his feet, cleared his throat, and announced in his high, jerky voice, "Helen and Harry, Medora and Suzita, Mona and Edwin, Willard and Dale, you are the nearest I have to a family of my own. I love you one and all. I know, Harry, that you disapprove of my drinking spirits here, but out of consideration for me you have made an exception; that alone would put me in your debt. Glasses up, then:

> Here's a health to all those that we love
> Here's a health to all those that love us,
> Here's a health to all those that love them that
> love those
> That love them that love those that love us.

"Drink water if you wish, drink milk or coffee, if that is all your palsied innards can handle; but drink!" And he tossed off his glass. Papa and Mama sipped from their water goblets. The younger children, trying to imitate their great-uncle, tried to glug down all their water at once, which resulted in an outbreak of coughing that went on for some time.

The discussion of Redlands as a possible alma mater

continued throughout the meal; Mama and Papa were taking the prospect seriously. Papa began to speculate about whether Mr. Clark, who had been operating the ranch as a tenant for several months past, would be able to keep it under control without supervision. If so, what should his compensation be? Mama looked wistful when Uncle Allie spoke of warm weather and orange groves. Clearly, the grown-ups were moving toward a consensus. Unfortunately, it was shattered when the hired girl brought in the dessert—dried apple pie. At the sight of the dish, Uncle Allie seemed to swell; his face reddened; I imagined that Author Unknown, beside him, swelled and reddened too. Uncle Allie pointed a shaking finger at the dessert on his plate and said incredulously, "Helen—do I find you doing this to me, your own uncle, the only uncle you have? Take it away—take it away!" He clapped his hands over his face as if to shut out the dreadful sight, and groaned through his fingers:

I loathe, abhor, despise,
Abominate dried apple pies.

I like good bread, I like good meat,
  Or anything that's fit to eat,
But of all the poor grub beneath the skies,
  The poorest is dried apple pies.
Give me the toothache or sore eyes
  In preference to such kind of pies.
Tread on my corns, or tell me lies,
But don't pass me dried apple pies!

Mama, whose sense of humor was on the shaky side, looked stricken. Papa, to whom Mama's peace and contentment were more precious than rubies, was furious.

"Alfred," he said, "I know your ways are not our ways—I have tried to make allowances. But you will apologize to Helen this instant—or—dad cuss it—you will leave this house right now."

Uncle Allie was momentarily bewildered, and then utterly contrite. "Helen!" he exclaimed. "I was making a joke—a joke, Helen! Don't you know I wouldn't hurt your feelings for the world?" He heaved himself to his feet and went to her, putting his incongruously thin arm about her shoulder. "Author Unknown and I *love* apple pies, Helen! Look!" Returning to his place, he bolted half his wedge of pie in a single great gulp, and tossed the rest to the dog, who caught it in midair and swallowed it.

Once he could speak after his massive feat of swallowing, Uncle Allie said, "You see? Author Unknown and I *love* apple pie!" And he went on:

When God had made the oak trees
  And the beeches and the pines,
  And the flowers and the grasses,
  And the tendrils of the vines,
He saw that there was wanting
A something in his plan,
  And he made the little apples,
  The little cider apples;
  The sharp, sour, cider apples,
To prove his love for man.

"That's the way we feel about apple pie," he concluded triumphantly. "Where is a second helping?"

The breach was repaired (though Papa's goatee continued to quiver for some time), and Ed and I wound up matriculating at Redlands in the fall.

The day after the pie incident was a Sunday. The family worshiped, as always, at the little church Grandpa Espy had donated to the local Baptists back in the nineties. For the first time, Uncle Allie came with us. His step was less light than usual; obviously he was still suffering from the effects of conscience and dried apple pie. He was so much on his best behavior that he did not insist on taking Author Unknown into the church, but instead left him on the stoop. The dog reflected his master's mood; he sat on command, and looked hangdog.

Uncle Allie would never have deliberately hurt anyone's feelings, I am sure. What happened at church that Sunday was simply a reaction to the apple pie incident. Subjectively speaking, he was changing the subject. Or perhaps he simply could not resist a joke.

He bowed his head during the prayers; he listened intently to the remarks of volunteer witnesses for the Lord (the church could not afford a paid minister); he stood when the rest of us stood, and sat when we sat. The first sign that his mood was lightening came when he whispered in my ear during a hymn,

Ech, sic a pairish, a pairish, a pairish,
  Ech, sic a pairish was little Kilkell:
They hae hangit the minister, droont the Precentor,
  They pu'd down the steeple, and drunkit the bell.

Papa loved to sing hymns. His powerful bass voice emerged with the roar of a river in spate, louder even than that of Henry Lehman, the Sunday school superintendent. There was only one trouble: Papa could not carry a tune. Once, when Papa and Mr. Lehman were trying to drown each other out in the "Rock of Ages," Uncle Allie put his mouth against my ear again to speak,

And when he sang in choruses
  His voice o'ertopped the rest,
Which is very inartistic,
  But the public like that best.

The presence of Mr. Anonymous in church caused heads to turn and elbows to jog among the congregation. When Mr. Lehman, as he did each week, called on all sinners to step forward and accept Jesus Christ as their redeemer, eyes inevitably swung to our pew. Uncle Allie, who was in the aisle seat, promptly arose.

"My friends," he squeaked, "here stands a poor, repentant sinner. I have drunk strong waters" (a gasp from the congregation); "I have lied" (another gasp); "I have fornicated" (the loudest gasp of all, almost a moan); "but on this day of glory, Jesus, I repent; I accept you; I kneel at your feet; I am yours!"

At this point he sidestepped into the aisle, and leaped into the air as I had seen him leap the first time I met him. He landed jigging, and singing high and sweet:

Oh, it's H–A–P–P–Y I am, and it's
  –F–R–double E,
And it's G–L–O–R–Y to know that I'm
  S–A–V–E–D.
Once I was B–O–U–N–D by the chains of
  S–I–N
And it's L–U–C–K–Y I am that all is
  well again.

Oh, the bells of Hell go ting-a-ling-a-ling
  For you, but not for me.
The bells of Heaven go sing-a-ling-a-ling
  For there I soon shall be.
Oh, Death, where is thy sting-a-ling-a-ling,
  Oh, Grave, thy victoree-e?
No ting-a-ling-a-ling, no sting-a-ling-a-ling,
  But sing-a-ling-a-ling for me.

He then subsided into the pew, where he sat with bowed head for the rest of the service. Afterward, he stood outside the church as dignified as a tombstone, and gravely shook the hands of well-wishers who filed by to congratulate him on his conversion. Author Unknown stood by as reverently immobile as a setter at point.

I cannot resist breaking the thread of my narrative here to say a few reminiscent words about Mr. Lehman, who almost wept as he shook Uncle Allie's hand. In his late sixties, Mr. Lehman was too good for this world. His belief in the Bible was unquestioning. In Sunday school class, I regularly and heartlessly brought up the question of how Jonah managed to survive three days in the belly of the whale, simply to hear Mr. Lehman thresh about, trying to find a rationale. He was too gentle to give me the thrashing I deserved.

To the best of my knowledge, Mr. Lehman was subject to only two of the million varieties of sin—and his two sins were venial. First, he fell from grace whenever he hired out Senith, his big brown horse, or Jenny, his small white mule. These beasts, which once had provided motive power for his mail wagon, now spent most of their time at pasture. Occasionally, however, some farmer needed one or both of them to pull a plow, a mowing machine, or a hay wagon. Mr. Lehman's sin was to bargain for their services as if they had been young Percherons.

Though Senith the horse and Jenny the mule no longer hauled the stage, he still used them for his own transportation, sitting behind them on the high seat of a buckboard wagon. They were unique in their viscousness of movement. If they had not used four legs apiece, one would have called their progress less a walk than a crawl. Mr. Lehman was proud that they both took defecation in stride. For urination, however, Jenny had to stop, and Senith had to stop with her. Since she suffered from a bladder ailment, the wagon came to a halt every two or three hundred yards. Mr. Lehman's features writhed in sympathy whenever Jenny strained to relieve herself. "Poor girl, poor girl," he would say to anyone about, "She'll be twenty-nine next November; ah well, we are all getting along."

The affinity between Senith, Jenny, and Mr. Lehman was a source of endless fascination to Uncle Allie. He used to speculate that perhaps Mr. Lehman was really not a man at all, but a reincarnation of Chiron the centaur. Once he even persuaded the gentle old man to memorize the first verse of a cowboy song:

My mammy was a blushing mare,
My old man was a stallion;
The half of me is centipede
And the rest of me is hellion;
For I'm a mule, a long-eared fool,
And I ain't never been to school.

A second verse went:

My mammy was a wall-eyed goat,
My old man was an ass,
And I feed myself off leather boots
And dynamite and grass;
For, etc.

Mr. Lehman refused to memorize the second verse, because he considered the word ass indelicate; but the first verse became his signature. When driving, he would crack his whip and sing lustily past his mutilated tongue (part of which had been removed as cancerous):

My mammy was a bluffing mare,
My ole man wav a ftallion . . .

Mr. Lehman's second sin was to call the reels at square dances. These took place on the first Saturday evening of every month in the grammar school.

Notable among them was one held on the Saturday following Mr. Anonymous's scandalously lighthearted marriage to Christ.

6

WHEREIN MR. ANONYMOUS YIELDS TO THE GRAPE AND PRACTICES THE ART OF SEDUCTION

Though I met Mr. Anonymous first in the summer of 1916, associated intimately with him for the next three years, and corresponded with him for seven years subsequently, I was still remarkably ignorant of the true man when he revisited Oysterville in July 1926. There was an elusive quality to Uncle Allie: He might put on a show for his public; he might jig on the streets; he might ostentatiously bring his palms to the ground without bending his knees; but the private person rarely emerged.

My growing compendium of his works hinted at more than I could understand. There were trenchant aphorisms; violent attacks on well-known personalities, political parties, even the structure of society; philosophical disquisitions; patriotic declamations; bitter satires; riddles; love poems that dripped. His works, like Goethe's, loomed as "fragments of a great confession." He contradicted himself from one tract to the next; he fluttered from the gay to the grave like a wren from branch to branch. He was a philistine: I remember his remarking once, "When I hear artists or authors making fun of businessmen I think of a regiment in which the band makes fun of the cook." He preferred the company of ignoramuses to that of pedants. Yet he was an informed and cultured man.

It was natural that his acquaintance with an odd little boy of five should have been based first on the subjects which interested the boy most—birds and animals, the sky and the sea. He may have felt it imperative to be my friend in order to become my preceptor. On that theory, his curious carryings-on at the community dance held at the Oysterville grammar school on Saturday, July 9, 1926 may have signalled a recognition of the new pumping in my own glands.

I was then, you will remember, at an age when my principal interest consisted of biting into the forbidden fruits of adolescence. Among these was strong drink. For two years past, my friend Roy Kemmer and I had made valiant efforts to ferment blackberries into wine, though the end product was always vinegar.

It happened that on the evening before the Oysterville dance Roy and I did manage to conjure up the devils that dwell in moonshine whiskey. We had persuaded our parents to let us visit Long Beach, a hurdy-gurdy summer resort between Ilwaco and Oysterville. Here we lay in wait at the entrance to the public dance hall. When between dances young men went to a nearby sand dune, dug up bottles of white mule they had secreted there, and treated themselves to a snort, Roy and I marked the burial place of the bottles. Once the owners were gone, we uncovered the bottles and manfully imbibed the whiskey, gagging and coughing between swallows. By the time we started home in Roy's pick-up truck, the outside world had lost reality for us. We drove through a flash-fire of blazing trees, one of which crashed across the road not a hundred feet behind our truck; next day I would have considered the event no more than a smoky, spark-filled nightmare, had not the fire been the talk of the peninsula. We arrived home at two in the morning; Mrs. Kemmer was still up, standing in the middle of the road to make us stop, beating the gravel with a long stick as a drummer might beat a drum. Next day we were under simultaneous attack from our consciences, our heads, and our families. Uncle Cecil is said to have commented that "Willard would be all right if only someone would keep after him with a pitchfork." Roy was denied permission to attend the community dance that evening, and I would have been kept home too if Uncle Allie had not interceded for me.

Mr. Lehman supervised the affair. He started the ceremonies by pumping air into two acetylene gas lanterns. After touching a match to the porous white mantles in which the gas burned, and settling the glass chimneys firmly in place, he hung the lanterns on hooks suspended from the ceiling. The light glared white, unlike the soft yellow of our usual coal oil lamps; whenever it dimmed, Mr. Lehman restored the glare by forcing air into a valve near the bottom of the lantern, using a smaller version of a bicycle pump. As the evening wore on, he pumped less often, and the room grew duskier.

Mr. Lehman roared out the reels. He beat the time with his heavy boots; his horny palms clapped together like board hitting board. His speech impediment imparted special piquancy to his callings; he would sing,

> We'll *hoop* the buffalo, we'll *hoop* the buffalo;
> We'll wander through the canebrake, and *hoop*
> the buffalo.

Years before, the fiddler had been an Indian with a peg leg. Nowadays, he was replaced by Jimmy Anderson, one of the bachelors (locally called hermits) who cultivated their garden patches in the woods around Oysterville. Jimmy, a gentle, slight little man with a stammer, accepted as an article of faith that the warped fiddle he had found in his mother's garret was a genuine Stradivarius. He regarded himself, with humble wonder, as a virtuoso who but for the vagaries of fate would have been a soloist at Carnegie Hall. When congratulated after clawing his way through Dvořák's "Humoresque," Jimmy hung his graying head, rubbed a boot on the floor, and whispered, "It must be just a g-g-g-gift, I g-g-g-guess."

Jimmy once confided to me that he spent much time reading poetry. When I asked him if he could remember any examples, the only lines he could quote were two that he attributed to Tennyson, though I happened to know the actual author well:

> The man sat in the gallery,
> His feet were in the orchestry.

Uncle Allie participated in the dancing with enthusiasm; his majestic stomach swayed, his spindly legs flew. He swung his ladies—particularly a flushed, comfortable-looking widow named Mrs. Calder—with vigor and finesse. The songs must have given him a particular, secret pleasure, knowing how many of them he had written:

Went down to milk and I didn't know how,
I milked the goat instead of the cow;
A monkey sittin' on a pile of straw
A-winkin' at his mother-in-law.
Roll 'em and twist 'em up a high tuckahaw
And hit 'em up a tune called "Turkey in the Straw."

His voice circled an octave over Mr. Lehman's when Jimmy played *Pop Goes the Weasel*:

Money for a spool of thread,
Money for a needle,
That's the way the money goes—
Pop goes the weasel!

I did not feel up to dancing; instead I sat and watched. At one point Uncle Allie hightailed over to me. He was sweating profusely; he rubbed his red kerchief between his collar and neck. His eyes bulged and shone behind their thick lenses. He was wearing the long-tailed blue jacket—resplendent with brass buttons—familiar from primary school days, and a pair of gray trousers so tight that his legs looked like a crane's. Author Unknown, who had been lying by the stove, pulled himself up, stretched, yawned, and joined us.

"Did you write *Pop Goes the Weasel*, Uncle Alfred?"

"Afraid not, Willard—just inherited it, so to speak."

"How can a weasel go pop?"

"Simple. England used to have a hatter's tool called a weasel, and 'pop' meant to pawn. When you popped your weasel, you pawned your hat."

"I read once that *Pop Goes the Weasel* was really written by a nineteenth-century composer named Mandale."

"Mandale!" Uncle Allie's squeak quivered with scorn. "Willard, you don't know the lengths to which some people will go to steal credit. You write something good, and it catches on, and people quote it, and sooner or later some silly muckhead will claim it was written by Bill Shakespeare or Peter Fiddle-dee-dee. *I* remember Mandale. He couldn't have popped a weasel out of a paper bag."

It was a frequently voiced vexation of Mr. Anonymous that other writers were constantly trying to claim his creations. Once a passage was attributed to him, he incorporated it into his persona, and refused thenceforth to release it, whether it belonged there or not.

To emphasize his last statement, he leaned toward me and waggled a finger the size of a Corona-Corona cigar. I noticed an odor about him that I had reason to recall from my own experience of the previous evening. I sniffed.

"Uncle Allie, have you been drinking?"

"Willard, my dear boy, are you criticizing me? *You*? *After last night*?"

"You have written a hundred times that every boy has to sow his wild oats. But *you* are a grown man, even older than Papa and Mama. I don't think they would like your drinking in public."

"In public? I haven't tasted a drop since I came in the door. Which reminds me—"

He fumbled for his hip pocket, from which he produced a familiar flask. I looked around hastily to see if anyone was watching.

"Don't you think we should go outside?" I asked.

"You are absolutely right, my boy," said Uncle Allie. "I predict great accomplishments for you in this world." He marched out the door. Author Unknown and I followed. Once in the yard, beyond range of the glaring lantern, he unscrewed the flask, tipped back his head, and let the liquor gush down his throat. Recapping the flask, he chuckled.

"Long before you were born," he said, "I visited an inn called the Beehive at Abingdon, in Berkshire. I paid for my drinks by lettering an inn-sign; no doubt it's there to this day. The words went like this:

Within this hive,
We're all alive,
Good liquor makes us funny,
So if you're dry,
Come in and try
The flavor of our honey.

"Do you find that amusing, Willard?"
"Mildly."
"Ah—the perennial perfectionist. Well, while we're on the subject of alcohol, how about this little epitaph?

He had his beer
From year to year
And then his bier had him.

It took a moment for the pun to penetrate, but then I said, "Oh yes, that's a good one."
Uncle Allie unscrewed his flask-cap again, swallowed, and recited:

There are several reasons for drinking,
And one has just entered my head;
If a man cannot drink when he's living
How the hell can he drink when he's dead?

At that moment the schoolhouse door opened and closed again. "Willard," said Uncle Allie softly, "did you happen to notice who just came out?"
"It looked like Mrs. Calder."
"Ah! Would that be the rather voluptuous little lady I squired in the Virginia reel?"
"Yes, and she seems to be coming this way. Shouldn't we move deeper into the shadow?"
"No, no," said Uncle Allie, rescrewing the cap, and tucking away the flask; "mustn't be impolite, my boy. She may want a word with me."
And indeed she did. "Mr. Richardson," she said, "is that you? Oh—of course it is. How do you do, Willard?"
"How do you do, Mrs. Calder?" said I.
"Author Unknown," said Uncle Allie, "say how-do-you-do to Mrs. Calder."
Author Unknown uttered a bark that was half a growl.
"Mr. Richardson, I have had no opportunity to tell you how moved I was—how much it meant to me, personally—last Sunday when you accepted Jesus Christ our Lord as your redeemer."
"And a newborn man I am," said Uncle Allie with fervor, "as a woman of your beauty and insight would

instantly recognize if we had but an opportunity to discuss the matter in private."

"A discussion of our dear Lord and Master is never out of place," said Mrs. Calder.

"One is less self-conscious away from the madding crowd," said Uncle Allie. "And the moon as big as a porridge plate, too. But aren't you chilly without your coat, my dear?"

"I rushed out without thinking," said Mrs. Calder. "I saw you leaving and was so afraid I might not catch you—"

"Willard," said Uncle Allie, "would you have the kindness to go fetch Mrs. Calder's coat, before the poor woman freezes?"

"It's belted, with a blue and white check," said Mrs. Calder.

"I'll be glad to," I said, and moved away. I was still within earshot when he remarked, "Not but what some women, my dear Mrs. Calder—Elly, if I may call you so—" ("Please do," she said.) "My dear Elly—and you must call me Allie—not but what some women, as I was saying, would be but the fairer the less they wore."

"Why, Mr. Richardson—I mean Allie—oh, dear, I am in such a flutter I don't know what I'm saying—how you do carry on!"

"I recall a line on that very subject" (and suddenly Uncle Allie's high voice was transformed into the cooing of a falsetto dove):

My love in her attire doth show her wit,
  It doth so well become her;
For every season she hath dressings fit,
  For winter, spring, and summer.
  No beauty she doth miss,
  When all her robes are on;
  But Beauty's self she is,
  When all her robes are gone.

"How you do carry on!" repeated Mrs. Calder.

I was almost out of earshot when I heard her say, "I know I'm silly, but big dogs do make me so nervous!"

Uncle Allie spoke with unaccustomed sharpness: "Home, Author Unknown. I said, *go home!*"

When I returned with the coat, there was no sign of Uncle Allie or Mrs. Calder. I looked around for a few moments, then returned to the dance. Who was it, I asked myself, who had described Samuel Johnson as "romantic about love, yet rakish about women"? Was it Boswell? Or could it have been Mr. Anonymous himself? Apparently, in any event, Uncle Allie fitted the description. Seduction, I was sure, was taking place somewhere nearby. The time had come, I told myself, to utilize in my own thinking the asterisks whose value my uncle had so carefully explained to me:

An author owned an asterisk
And kept it in his den
Where he wrote tales which had large sales
Of erring maids and men,
And always, when he reached the point
Where carping censors lurk,
He called upon the asterisk
To do his dirty work.

Surely, I argued with myself, my imagination must be running out of bounds. Uncle Allie was past sixty-five. Mrs. Calder was a deaconess of the church. Sixty-five! Deaconess! Unaccountably, my own libido, ordinarily ablaze at this point in a sociable evening, was utterly quiescent.

Inside, I danced a reel halfheartedly with my sister Mona, now twenty-one, who smiled over my head at other boys dancing with other girls. I even ventured to trip a toe, fantastic if not light, with Alice Sargent. But my mind was otherwise engaged. I seated myself by an open window idly regarding the dancers.

Of special interest to me was a tall young man, perhaps eighteen, fair and even-featured, with a dotted bow tie that bobbed on his Adam's apple like a butterfly about to flutter away. He danced reel after reel, each time with a different partner. One of my friends, perhaps Roy, had informed me that this particular youth was very conscious of a private paucity. Years later Mr. Anonymous wrote a clerihew applicable to such problems:

Didorous Siculus
Made himself ridiculous,
He thought a thimble
Was the phallic symbol.

But I could not get Uncle Allie and the widow Calder out of my mind. Eventually I slipped outside again, moving as quietly as I could through the underbrush surrounding the school yard. At length I heard an unmistakable falsetto whisper:

Sweet Cupid, ripen her desire,
Thy joyful harvest may begin;
If age approach a little nigher,
'Twill be too late to get it in.

Cold winter storms lay standing corn,
Which once too ripe will never rise,
And lovers wish themselves unborn,
When all their joys lie in their eyes.

Then, sweet, let us embrace and kiss;
Shall beauty shale upon the ground?
If age bereave us of this bliss,
Then will no more such sport be found.

There followed a rustling, and then a woman's hoarse, suppliant voice: "Oh no John! No John! No John! No."

But those could not have been the words I heard. Certainly the name was not John. The rustling continued, accompanied by muffled animal-like sounds. I wanted to leave, but my muscles refused to move. At last I heard Uncle Allie murmur contentedly:

"Ah, Elly, you're one in a million. Nor have I ever heard reluctance better put on."

"What do you mean by that, dear?"

"Why, you put me in mind for a while there of a poem I learned a long time ago—and never forget, a poem is what you are to me, my dear:

Sweet, let me go! Sweet, let me go!
What do you mean to vex me so?
Cease your pleading force!
Do you think thus to extort remorse?
Now, now! no more! alas, you overbear me,
And I would cry—but some would hear, I fear
me. . . .

"Surely, my dear, you did not expect a good Christian woman to yield to you at the first crook of your finger?"

"Certainly not, my dear Elly."

"Nor would I have let you so much as hold my hand had I not known you were a man of honorable intent."

Another silence. Then Uncle Allie said in a surprised tone:

"Veers the wind *never* from that quarter?" He piped plaintively:

Early one morning, just as the sun was rising,
I heard a maid sing in the valley below:
"Oh, don't deceive me; oh, never leave me!
How could you use a poor maiden so?"

"But *you* would never deceive me. We're *engaged* now, darling!"

There was something sadly *déjà vu* about all this. It brought to mind scores of verses I had heard from the lips of Mr. Anonymous—verses like this one:

Spring is hard on us;
Summer in bed we muss;
Fall the exploding beast;
Winter, post-coital trist.

I tiptoed back to the dance, away from the murmuring voices. Twenty minutes later Mrs. Calder entered the room, her hair and lace-collared green dress a trifle disheveled. The expression on her face made me glad I was not a cat close enough for her to kick. She plumped herself down at the other end of my bench, glaring at the revellers. Once in a while she muttered under her breath. Her hands clenched and unclenched as if she were milking a cow. Soon, from just outside the window there came a song so soft that it must have been intended for only her ears and mine:

We're a' dry wi' the drinkin' o't,
We're a' dry wi' the drinkin' o't,
The minister kissed the fiddler's wife,
And he couldna preach for thinkin' o't.

Mrs. Calder leaped as if she had sat on a pin and spun about, her hands in two tight fists. "You!" she shouted. "You dreadful—" Then she realized that her voice was overriding Henry Lehman's reel-calling, and broke off. A soft chant came again from the yard:

Some men want youth, and others health,
Some want a wife, and some a punk,
Some men want wit, and others wealth,
But they want nothing that are drunk.

The briefest of pauses, and then:

Would you be a man of fashion,
Would you lead a life divine?
Take a little dram of passion
In a lusty dose of wine.

If the nymph has no compassion,
Vain it is to sigh and groan.
Love was but put in for fashion,
Wine will do the work alone.

Mrs. Calder clapped her hands to her ears, her face crimson, and scurried to the other side of the room.

Uncle Allie was apparently erring aimlessly and drunkenly about the school yard, singing whatever occurred to him; had he been a dog, I would have said he was baying the moon. Once the words went:

I have no pain, dear Mother, now,
But oh, I am so dry;
So connect me to a brewery,
And leave me there to die.

Again, farther off:

He grabbed me round my slender neck,
I could not shout or scream,
He carried me into his room
Where we could not be seen;
He tore away my flimsy wrap
And gazed upon my form—
I was so cold and still and damp,
While he was wet and warm.
His feverish mouth he pressed to mine—
I let him have his way—
He drained me of my very self,
I could not say him nay.
He made me what I am. Alas!
That's why you find me here—
A broken vessel—broken glass
That once held bottled beer.

And again:

Would you like to sin
With Elinor Glyn
On a tiger skin?
Or would you prefer
To err with her
On some other fur?*

Nobody but me, and possibly Mrs. Calder, seemed to notice the outside competition with Jimmy's fiddle and Mr. Lehman's calling. The singing came again, this time harmonizing with the howl of a dog:

The horse and mule live 30 years
And nothing know of wines and beers.
The goat and sheep at 20 die
And never taste of Scotch or Rye.
The cow drinks water by the ton
And at 18 is mostly done.

* The novelist Elinor Glyn was still considered daring in the 1920s.

The dog at 15 cashes in
Without the aid of rum and gin.
The cat in milk and water soaks
And then in 12 short years it croaks.
The modest, sober, bone-dry hen
Lays eggs for nogs, then dies at 10.
All animals are strictly dry;
They sinless live and swiftly die;
But sinful, ginful, rum-soaked men
Survive for three score years and ten.
And some of them, a very few,
Stay pickled till they're 92.

And finally:

Come, landlord, fill the flowing bowl
Until it doth run over:
For tonight we'll merry merry be,
For tonight we'll merry merry be,
For tonight we'll merry be,
Tomorrow we'll be sober.

Gradually the stomping and the fiddling and the calling slowed to a stop. The dancers retrieved their wraps from the hat rack. Mona called that she was leaving, but I shook my head, and she went without me. Groups, couples, and singles drifted out the door. Mr. Lehman blew out the acetylene lanterns, and began on the kerosene lamps. I seemed unable to bestir myself; I might have gone to sleep right where I sat had I not heard a whine and felt a nuzzling against my thigh. Author Unknown had come to herd me home. Half-asleep, I followed him out the door, through the yard, up the lane, and across the street. There, under the lantern that lighted the porch gate of our house, Uncle Allie lay snoring, a supine Colossus of Rhodes. Author Unknown slowly paced my uncle's great length as if measuring it. Occasionally he paused to sniff. When he reached Uncle Allie's face he began to lick his cheeks, rolling bulging eyes helplessly at me the while. Uncle Allie snored louder. I shook his shoulder.

"Uncle Allie! Uncle Allie!" I begged, low and desperate,

as fearful of waking the family as of not waking Mr. Anonymous: "Wake up! Wake up! You've got to get to bed!"

His lips moved; a faint sound emerged:

> Thou swear'st thou'lt drink no more; kind
> heaven, send
> Me such a cook or coachman, but no friend!

I cannot remember how we accomplished it. Somehow I got him to a sitting position—to his knees—to his feet. He moved, one foot past the other, an arm around my shoulders and another around Author Unknown's. If common sense had not told me better, I would have sworn the dog was walking upright, like a man. We guided Uncle Allie into the house and felt our way through the darkened living room and library. As we passed the family room we still called the nursery, Papa called from behind the closed door, "Is that you, Willard? Is that you, Allie?"

"That's us, Papa," I called back. "Don't let the fleas bite!"

I never saw Mr. Anonymous drunk again.

7

WHEREIN MR. ANONYMOUS PROVIDES MORAL INSTRUCTION

My parents could not understand why Uncle Allie, after his spectacular conversion to Christ on the previous Sunday, refused to attend church on the morning following the dance, or why he announced that he had to cut his visit short and was leaving via Mr. Lehman's stage next day. When pressed for an explanation, he said only, "I had a dream telling me I must go."

One suspects that he had no intention of being around if Mrs. Calder accused him, publicly or privately, of having misled her, perhaps even undone her. If that was his fear, it was groundless; as far as I know, she remained silent until her dying day on whatever may have passed between her and Uncle Allie that Saturday night.

So Uncle Allie left for Redlands. Two months later we followed him by car. The Redlands area, then a sultry land of orange and citrus groves, was oppressive at first to a family from the damps of Oysterville; but we settled contentedly in an inexpensive cottage near the campus. Edwin and I registered as freshmen at the college; Dale attended the local high school.

Ed, sunnier, more outgoing, and far more conscientious than I, was marked even in his first months as a campus leader *in ovo*. He went on to fulfill his destiny. I, on the other hand, trying desperately to seem older than my fifteen years, pretended to a sophistication I did not possess, particularly in the area of relations between the sexes. My ego never quite recovered from a coed's report to one of my fraternity brothers that "Willard gets so excited in the car that he steams up all the windows, but then he never knows what to do." Looking back, it astonishes me that I had any amorous success at all; why should girls of eighteen or more have yielded to the importunities of a fifteen-year-old boy? Occasionally I thought I was in love; occasionally there may have been girls who thought briefly that they were in love with me. I exchanged poems with one such through the columns of the campus newspaper, until she found I was going out on the side with a round-heeled flibbertygibbet. She contributed one final poem to the exchange; I still wince, remembering the concluding lines:

. . . And then I saw you stoop to worship her,
One cheap as dust, and as available.
You became one with all you worshiped—you
who were
For one brief hour inviolable.

I believe that girl would have become a genuine poet had she not died of tuberculosis—the break between us still unmended three years later.

As a freshman, I was interested in drinking Virginia Dare wine and home-brewed beer; in playing poker at the Pi Chi fraternity which I was to join the following year; in attending dances; in slipping girls into their dormitories after hours; and in running up debts—trifling debts by today's standards, amounting at most to a half dollar or a dollar, but oppressive then. Uncle Allie, faculty advisor to Pi Chi, staked me occasionally, but insisted on being repaid. He never, however, took any of my possessions for collateral, though he claimed to have done this with borrowers at the University of Edinburgh before the turn of the century. There were so many spendthrifts among the supposedly canny Scots, he told me, that he had adapted an ancient refrain to describe them:

A stoodent A has gone and spent,
With a hey-lililu and a how-low-lan
All his money to a Cent,
And the birk and the broom blooms bonny.

His Creditors he could not pay,
With a hey-lililu and a how-low-lan,
And Prison proved a shock to A,
And the birk and the broom blooms bonny.

❧

My approach to life became less deplorable after my sophomore year. I remained, however, a shallow scholar.

My parents watched me perhaps less closely than they should have, knowing that Uncle Allie was on campus to keep me on the straight and narrow. In at least one area, however, my uncle tended rather to abet than to abort my worst adolescent impulses. My singing has always been in the tuneless tradition of my father. When I wished to serenade some dormitory maiden, therefore, I enlisted Uncle Allie's aid, as Christian in similar circumstances called on Cyrano de Bergerac. We would stand hidden in the shadows beneath the dormitory window; I would whistle or toss gravel until I received some signal of awareness from the object of my attentions; and she would listen, along probably with the girls in all the rooms around, as I mimed under the arc light, while Uncle Allie in the darkness behind me sang love in his high voice. His favorites were such songs as:

My little pretty one,
My pretty honey one,
She is a jolly one
And gentle as can be.
With a beck she comes anon.
With a wink she will be gone.
No doubt she is alone
Of all that ever I see.

Or:

She was brighter of her blee
  than was the bright sonn;
Her rudd redder than the rose
  that on the rise hangeth;
Meekly smiling with her mouth,
  and merry in her lookes.
Ever laughing for love,
  as she like would.
And as she came by the bankes,
  the boughes each one
They louted to that ladye,
  and layd forth their branches;

Blossoms, and burgens
breathed full sweet;
Flowers flourished in the frith,
where she forth stepped;
And the grasse, that was gray,
greened belive.

This charade seldom succeeded in its basic purpose, which was to win the girl involved; but it had a side effect. Professor Olds, head of the music department, hearing that an unexploited vocal talent was loose in the school, asked me to try out for the choir. Like Papa before me, I must have had no idea how badly I sang, for I quickly agreed. On the day of my first and last rehearsal, Professor Olds heard all the aspirants through one chorus of "Oh That Dear Old U. of R." Then he held up his hand.

"Something is wrong here," he said. "I want those of you on the right-hand side of the aisle to stop singing, and we'll go through the lines again."

The second rendition gave him a clue. "All right," he said. "Now you in the first three rows on the left keep quiet, and you in the last three sing."

I was in the last row, and I sang with a will—such a will that the professor instantly identified my monotone. "You," he said, pointing his baton at me; "I suggest that you leave the musical world, and take up debating."

I took the first half of the suggestion.

I recall that I wore my bathrobe over my pajamas to my first class each morning. I must have returned home after the class to dress, for it was obligatory to attend morning chapel. President Duke, a dark-faced, white-haired man of commanding presence, large-framed and towering over most of his students, was not noted for laxity; surely he would not have stood for a student worshiping in nightgear. Even as it was, when Dr. Duke strode past my group on the way to or from chapel, he invariably said, "Good morning, gentlemen and Mr. Espy," which was not meant as flattery.

Besides English, my language studies at one time or another included Latin, French, Spanish, and German. My conduct in these, as in all other classes, was inexcusable. My Spanish professor suspended me for a week when I chose for my daily recitation a work of Mr. Anonymous that happened to be on my mind because he had recited it to me only the night before:

There once was a Filipino *hombre*
Who ate rice, *pescado y legumbre,*
His trousers were wide and his shirt hung outside,
And this, I may say, was *costumbre.*

He lived in a *nipa bajai*
Which served as a stable and sty,
And he slept on the mat with the dogs and a cat,
And the rest of the family nearby.

His *mujer* once kept a *tienda*
Underneath a large stone *hacienda*;
She chewed betel and sold for jawbone and gold
To *soldados* who said "*No intienda.*"

Su hermana fué lavandera
And slapped clothes in *fuerta manera*
On a rock in the stream where *carabaos* dream,
Which gave them a perfume *lifera.*

Of *niños* he had *dos* or *tres*
Good types of the tagalog race;
In dry or wet weather, in the altogether,
They'd romp and they'd race and they'd chase.
When his *pueblo* last had a *fiesta*
His *familia* tried to digesta
Mule which had died of glanders inside—
Y ahora su familia no esta!*

Uncle Allie instructed me in Italian on the side. To demonstrate that any condition of nature could sound beautiful given the proper words, he taught me one of

* For non-speakers of Spanish, I perhaps should explain that *pescado y legumbre* are fish and vegetables; *nipa bajai,* a house of nipa palm fronds; *mujer,* a woman; *tienda,* a store; "*No intienda,*" "I don't know"; *Su hermana fué lavandera,* his sister was a laundress; *fuerta manera,* briskly; *carabaos,* water oxen; *lifera,* rank; *niños,* children; *dos,* two; *tres,* three; *pueblo,* town; *fiesta,* celebration; and *Y ahora su familia no esta* (the esta should be está; it is mispronounced for the rhyme), Now his family is no more.

his own Italian creations. I asked my Spanish professor to let me recite it in class. She agreed, and the sound was indeed as beautiful as I had promised:

Strunz' . . .
Nel sole fumante
Com'è un incenso
A Dio . . .
Una mosca
Ti canta
Una ninna-nanna . . .
Zzz . . . Zzz . . .
Ma . . . tu non ascolti . . .
Strunz' . . .

"Lovely!" said Miss Hill. "Can you translate it?"

"Oh," I said vaguely, "it's about a boy who is praying God to make a beautiful woman listen to him." Fortunately, she inquired no further. The actual English rendition would be, "Turd, smoking in the sun to God like a censer . . . A fly sings you a hush-a-bye . . . Zzz . . . Zzz . . . but . . . you don't listen . . . Turd!"

My Latin teacher, Professor Kyle, would forgive me any impudence or imprudence as long as it had a Latin twist. Mr. Anonymous armed me with a number of macaronic verses, for which I always received an A grade in Latin, though they lost me the benefits of Cicero and Vergil. This illiterate sample sticks in my mind:

Puer ex Jersey
Iena ad school;
Vidit in meadow,
Infestum mule.

Ille approaches
O magnus sorrow!
Puer it skyward.
Funus ad morrow.

MORAL:

Qui vidit a thing
None ei well-known,
Est bene for him
Relinqui id alone.

Professor Kyle even welcomed macaronics in which Latin played only a minor part. Mr. Anonymous wrote one, for instance, in five languages—English for the first line of each stanza, French for the second, German for the third, Latin for the fourth, and Italian for the fifth:

There once was a frolicsome flea
Son chien lui dépluit comme abri
  Er Wollt' einen Kater
  Sed observat mater
Non lasci i parenti così.

But he listened not to their prayer
Il quittá son père et sa mère,
  Er springt' auf 'ne Katze
  Sed haec rasitat se
Lo mangi, orribile a veder.

Around and about the gore flew
Aie pitié du petit fou
  Mit lautem Geschrei
  Vae mihi, o vae,
Il povero accese in giù.

The moral of this little tale:
Ne tentez la force de vos ailes
  Bleib' ruhig zu Haus
  Sit domui laus
Alla casa dimora fidel.

I provided a liberal translation that pleased Professor Kyle and, more importantly, Mr. Anonymous:

A Flea, bored with Dog as a diet,
Heard of Cat, and decided to try it.
He cried, "Let me go,"
But his parents said, "No!
Stay at home on our Dog and keep quiet."

The Flea didn't heed them a mite
He jumped on a Cat for a bite.
This maddened the Puss,
Who scratched the flea loose
And ate him—a horrible sight.

⁂

The dying flea popped with a splat—
Oh, pity the poor little brat,
Crying, "Mom, take me back!"
As, alas and alack,
He slides down the throat of the cat.

My Moral, dear friend, is a hot one:
What seems like a snack may be not one;
If you live on pup,
Stay at home and shut up;
Be glad of a home if you've got one.

A few nights later, Mr. Anonymous said to me: "Here is food for thought, Willard. Some time ago, one of my Yiddish counterparts wrote a verse that went:

Wenn der Rabbi trennt,
Schocklen sich die Wend,
Und alle Hassidim,
Kleppen mit die Hend."

"What does that mean?" I asked.

"Roughly, 'When the Rabbi has marital intercourse, the walls shake, and all the Hassidim clap their hands.' "

"I can do a better version than that," I said. "The translation should be:

Rabbi, when you fill her gap,
All the walls go flippy-flap;
All the grave Hassidim clap."

"Willard," said Uncle Alfred, "you have possibilities."

The University of Redlands dates from 1910, and Pi Chi is its first-born fraternity.

It was good for the Pi Chi image to obtain Edwin as a pledge; he was religiously bent and obviously headed for high estate on campus. To acquire him, they were willing to take me too. I was not a Big Athlete, a Big Man About Campus, a Big Man with the Women, or even a Big Brain; but at least I could hold my own at poker against such wily opponents as Carroll Montague, Bob Whiteside, Clint McKinnon, and Al Johnson.

As Uncle Allie put it, aping Shakespeare:

> To draw or not to draw,—that is the question:—
> Whether 'tis safer in the player to take
> The awful risk of skinning for a straight,
> Or, standing pat, to raise 'em all the limit
> And thus, by bluffing, get in. To draw—to skin;
> No more—and by that skin to get a full,
> Or two pairs, or the fattest bouncing kings
> That luck is heir to—'tis a consummation
> Devoutly to be wished—

I did not exactly cheat at these games, but I kept Author Unknown at my side, and came to suspect that the sequence of thumps given off by his tail constituted suggestions to pass, raise, or call. My winnings at penny ante were regarded with envy by my fraternity brothers, some of whom were so distrustful as to hint that I marked the decks.

Each fraternity had a faculty advisor. Uncle Allie was ours. His irreverence for most codes held sacred at Redlands made him an object of suspicion among the more conservative professors, but at least he saw to it that we did not consume alcoholic beverages or entertain girls at the fraternity house. His nose for concealed wine, beer, or whiskey was infallible; or perhaps it was Author Unknown who did the sniffing. Our conduct off premises, however, was our own business. Uncle Allie asked no troublesome questions when Pi Chis travelled sixty miles, on mischief bent, to Los Angeles, or even a hundred plus miles to Tijuana, across the Mexican border. In both places liquor and other forbidden entertainment were readily available. Though it was his responsibility to accompany us as chaperon, he generally absented himself on his own matters until the time came to start back to Redlands.

Yet Uncle Allie talked constantly about the joys of alcohol, and encouraged us to do the same. This was probably one reason ours was considered the most wicked social organization on campus. Uncle Allie went so far as to insist that every pledge memorize an anonymous saying: "Good wine maketh good blood; good blood causeth good humors; good humors cause good thoughts; good thoughts bring forth good works; good works carry a man to heaven. Ergo, good wine carrieth a man to heaven."

He taught us to sing with a will (to the tune of "This Old Man, He Played One"):

Beaujolais! Beaujolais!
Appellation controlée!
Beaujolais est joli, joli beau—
Bonne santé, and cheerio!

If our drinking song was not "Beaujolais," it might be:

Take me down, down, down where the Würz-
burger flows, flows, flows,
Let me drown, drown, drown, all my troubles
and woes, woes, woes;
Just order two seidels of lager, or three,
If I don't want to drink it, please force it on me.
The Rhine may be fine
But a cold stein for mine,
Down where the Würzburger flows.

I alone realized that these old drinking songs were the personal creations of Professor Alfred Richardson of the Department of Languages. This secret knowledge increased by euphoria as the brothers knocked their glasses of near beer together.

Sometimes Uncle Allie would rap on the table for silence, bounce to his feet with that agility which never ceased to astonish me, and address us as follows:

I beg you come tonight and dine.
A welcome waits you, and sound wine,—
The Roederer chilly to a charm,
As Juno's breath the claret warm,
The sherry of an ancient brand.
No Persian pomp, you understand—
A soup, a fish, two meats, and then
A salad fit for aldermen

(When aldermen, alas the days!
Were really worth their *mayonnaise*);
A dish of grapes whose clusters won
Their bronze in Carolinian sun;
Next, cheese: for you the Neufchatel,
A bit of Cheshire likes me well;
Café au lait or coffee black,
With Kirsch or Kummel or cognac,
Cigars and pipes. These being through,
Friends shall drop in, a very few—
Shakespeare and Milton, and no more.
When these are guests I bolt the door,
With "Not at home" to anyone
Excepting Alfred Tennyson.

Another of his songs, doubtless still being sung at Pi Chi revels to this day, went:

I cannot eat but little meat,
   My stomach is not good;
But sure I think that I can drink
   With him that wears a hood.
Though I go bare, take ye no care,
   I nothing am a-cold;
I stuff my skin so full within
   Of jolly good ale and old.

CHORUS:

Back and side go bare, go bare;
Both feet and hands go cold;
But, belly, God send thee good ale enough,
Whether it be new or old.

The song ran on interminably.

Another of Uncle Allie's oddities did not raise the reputation of either the fraternity or its advisor. He insisted on reciting a passage from *Holinshed's Chronicles* at every annual Pi Chi banquet. He delivered it slowly, carefully, squeakily, and with emphasis:

Irish Whiskey

It drieth up the breaking out of hands and killeth the flesh wormes, if you wash your hands therewith. It scowreth all scrufe and scalds from the head, being therewith dailie washt before meals. Being moderatelie taken it sloweth age, it strengtheneth you, it helpeth digestion, it cutteth flegm, it abandoneth melancholie, it relisheth the heart, it lighteneth the mind, it quickeneth the spirits, it cureth the hydropsie, it healeth the Strangurie, it pounceth the stone, it expelleth gravell, it puffeth awaie all ventositie, it keepeth and preserveth the head from whirling, the eies from dazeling, the Toong from lisping, the mouth from maffling, and the heart from swelling, the bellie from wirtching, the guts from numbing, the hands from shivering, and the sinewes from shrinking, the veines from srumpling, the bones from aking and the marrow from soaking. Ulstadius also ascribeth thereto a singular praise and would have it to burne being kindled which he taketh to be a token to know the goodness thereof. And trulie it is a sovereigne liquore if it be orderlie taken.

Uncle Allie generally taught only advanced language classes, and then only in the afternoon, except for one morning class in Greek. It was said that in this class he could instantly diagnose a hangover, and would send the sufferer home with this admonition:

Last evening you were drinking deep,
So now your head aches. Go to sleep;
Take some boil'd cabbage when you wake;
And there's an end of your headache.

Limericks, a popular verse form among Pi Chis, found little favor with Uncle Allie. He insisted that midden heaps of witless, off-color specimens had quite buried the few great examples of the genre, and admitted responsibility for only a handful of the thousands of limericks printed in his name.

"I have enemies, Willard," he would say; "there are

those who would do anything to sully my spotless reputation. Why, some anthologists even claim I wrote this:

Anon., Idem, Ibid. and Trad.
Wrote much that is morally bad:
  Some ballads, some chanties,
  All poems on panties—
And limericks, too, one must add."

"It happens that I am well acquainted with Idem, Ibid., and Trad.—all very fine fellows; you will meet them some day—and I can assure you that none of them would stoop, any more than I would, to composing most of the limericks attributed to them."

Perhaps as often as once a year, Mr. Anonymous would slip away for a reunion with Idem, Ibid., and Trad. He never told me what went on at those affairs, but he invariably returned with a headache that lasted for days.

8

WHEREIN MR. ANONYMOUS DISCUSSES POETRY

The campus newspaper was so hungry for copy that it would print virtually anything. In my drive for sexual conquest, I inundated the columns with poetry. I had to, for I lacked such other sexual bait as athletic prowess, symmetry of feature and form, or campus leadership. At least my effusions rhymed and scanned; free verse was the order of the day, but I managed to avoid that ultimate heresy. That the verses lack intellectual content was inevitable, since I had nothing to say.

Here is a typical example:

> You thought to hold a mirror to the world
>   Of men and things;
> To glimpse reflected glory, half-unfurled,
>   Of angel wings.
>
> But in your mirror, turn it as you might,
> Right ever changed to left, and left to right.

One after another of my verses continued in the same vein:

> Across the long years' interlude
>   What raptures will my spirit feign?
> What furtive pride in little gain
>   Replace my joyous certitude?
>
> Can this proud greatness I have bruited
>   Be born of tawdry self-delusion?
> These talents, sprung in green profusion,
>   Die in a day, too shallow-rooted?

❧§❧

O rosary of mumbling monk,
I too shall count a rosary:
"My goal shrank here," the chant will be,
"And here—and here—my goal has shrunk."

Not God, with angels girded 'bout,
Can ease this fear of counterfeit;
What though the heavens sanction it?
Not heaven, but myself I doubt.

The name Maitena was the ultimate in romance to me, and I applied it to anyone I was wooing:

What clay-foot idol kneelest thou before,
Maitena, when the hour of prayer is come?
What counsel wouldst thou have? My lips are dumb . . .
What benediction? I can bless no more.

No thaumaturge to exorcise this cold
Quiescence, O Maitena, canst thou find
A sun to light my eyes? Maitena, I am blind . . .
A song to bring me dreams? Maitena, I am old.

And I find this in my college files:

Contented the flesh, and resigned,
Uncaring what dawn may portend;
But—"Quick! we are nearing the end;
Oh, make haste!" cries the sensual mind;
"Ah, make haste!" sobs the prescient mind.

Mr. Anonymous snorted over these efforts; his face turned as red as a boiled lobster; he uttered incoherent sounds that might have indicated either disgust or laughter. But he refused to suggest how I might improve my writing.

"I am not God, boy," he would say. "If it is to happen, it will happen."

He respected me more for having read his macaronic and his Strunz tour de force in Spanish class than for any of my own writings. My love poems disturbed him most.

❧

It was a convention of the day to apostrophize one's beloved, and I followed the convention faithfully. One afternoon Uncle Allie tapped the college newspaper in which I had immortalized my latest Amaryllis, and inquired, "Willard, you don't really believe that this girl is so different from all the rest, do you?"

"Cora? Certainly she is."

"But in the last six months alone you must have applied comparable superlatives to at least half a dozen of the creatures."

"Creatures" seemed an invidious epithet.

"And you will agree that every one of them, with the possible exception of your current Cora, is now running around with other boys quite as happily as if you had never existed?"

There could be no doubt about that.

"Nor do I hear you mourning over Ella, or Tina, or Rose, or Mary, now that your attention is fixed on Cora."

"Uncle Allie, Cora is the gentlest, kindest—"

"Of course she is. Basically, though, isn't she the momentary incarnation of your Maitena? Set aside for the moment the fact that even Maitena seems to be simply a convenient target at which you can pitch your shallow emotions. In Cora's basic physical arrangements—mind you, I am not discussing such fine details as the curve of an eyelash—may I assume that she is much like any other girl? May I assume that Cora's field had been plowed, harrowed, even seeded and manured, before you and your extraordinary collection of farming equipment arrived?"

I disagreed most heartily; but on reflection I had to admit that perhaps my love poems tended toward the saccharine. So I was pleased the next time I visited Uncle Allie to read him a verse I had found it inadvisable to publish:

Seek not beauty; seek not wit;
Seek not wealth, or but a bit.
Seek instead the maiden who
Seeks no other man but you.
She will be when you are gone
Loyalty's own paragon.

❧§❧

She her virtue well will shield,
And, when she cannot but yield,
For one moment, maybe two,
May pretend that He is You.

Mr. Anonymous listened, a thumb pressed into the wattles under his chin. "Well!" he said cryptically. "Well! The sap begins to flow."

An exchange a few days later, though it began idly, brought about a lasting change in the relationship between me and Mr. Anonymous.

I had been sitting in what he called his easy chair—the one with a coiled spring thrusting through the fabric at the center of the seat. I was reading Andrew Marvell aloud:

The grave's a fine and private place,
But none, I think, do there embrace.

Suddenly my mind quaked. It flashed back a dozen years, to an instant in the Oysterville marshes when I dared not move, knowing something portentous was about to occur. As then, I held my breath outside a magical pentagon from which smoke was beginning to rise. As then, Uncle Allie and Author Unknown regarded me, waiting for some signal. But all I could say now was, "I do wish he'd said the *tomb*'s a fine and private place."

Uncle Allie cleared his throat.

"Why *tomb* rather than *grave*, my boy?"

"It would make such a nice takeoff! Listen:

The womb's a fine and private place
In which to propagate the race."

Uncle Allie said, almost grumpily, "Well, there you are. It took you longer than I had hoped, but you had to come around sooner or later."

I had no idea of what he was talking about. "Come around to what?"

"Never mind—never mind. You'll know soon enough." He brushed the back of his hand across his forehead; for a second I fancied the gesture had wiped an oddly forlorn expression from his face. "Anyhow, you are beginning to show signs of growing up."

I was sixteen and felt pretty grown-up already. "What do you mean, Uncle Allie?"

"Not to offend you, my boy, but I've noticed a tendency in you to take our literary poobahs at whatever valuation your professors placed on them. I'd be the last to denigrate the work of an established author, having, as you know, something of a reputation of my own" (here he puffed out his enormous belly as he always did when he thought he was puffing out his chest); "but you must come to recognize the defects inherent in other writers' virtues—love them more for the defects—see how easily imitators can turn those very virtues *into* defects by conscious or unconscious exaggeration."

He was talking over my head.

"Your Andrew Marvell couplet," he went on, "is called in the trade a parody, or burlesque. I myself find it instructive to burlesque well-known authors to bring out their essential style."

He made his way to a corner of the room heaped with cardboard boxes. When he had located the one he was looking for, he began to untie the cord that secured it. The knot presented considerable difficulty, and finally he had to cut it with a butcher knife. He then turned the box upside down. Yellowed clippings fluttered to the floor like leaves from a tree in an autumn windstorm. He picked up one of them.

"Take Herman Melville," he said. "There was a writer who was well enough in his early days. But he strangely mistook his own powers and the patience of his friends. He presumes to leave his native element, the ocean, and his original business of harpooning whales, for the mysteries and ambiguities of metaphysics, love, and romance. Here is a little takeoff on his later style that I did for *Godey's Lady's Book*:

> Melodiously breathing an inane mysteriousness, into the impalpable airiness of our unsearchable sanctum, this wonderful example of its ineffable author's sublime-winging imagination has been flut-

tering its snow-like-invested pinions upon our multitudinous table. Mysteriously breathing an inane melody, it has been beautifying the innermost recesses of our visual organs with the luscious purpleness and superb goldness of its exterior adornment. We have listened to its outbreathing of sweet-swarming sounds, and their melodious, mournful, wonderful, and unintelligible melodiousness has 'dropped like pendulous, glittering icicles,' with soft-ringing silveriness, upon your never-to-be-delighted sufficiently organs of hearing; and, in the insignificant significancies of that deftly-stealing and wonderfully-serpentining melodiousness, we have found an infinite, unbounded, inexpressible mysteriousness of nothingness."

"You see," Uncle Allie concluded, "what I accomplished? I have shown Melville in caricature. I have warned his imitators: So far, but no farther."

"Oh," said I.

"Where an author has lost perspective on his own work," he continued, "he can count on me to remind him. Some, though, are thicker-skinned than others. Take Walt Whitman—I must have done a hundred brilliant parodies on Whitman, give or take a dozen, and he never noticed them. This one, all by itself, should have been enough to bring him to his senses:

> I find that I am a more important person than I thought.
> I make the President, and the Governor, and the Judge on the bench, and the street-cleaning commissioner.
> If the President wishes to declare war, or to make peace, or to keep or not to keep the Philippine Islands, he waits to hear what I have to say.
> I am the President, and the Governor, and the Judge on the bench, and the street-cleaning commissioner.
> I find that when Ethan Allen captured Fort Ticonderoga, "in the name of Almighty God and the Continental Congress," and that when "Mad

Anthony" stormed the breastworks at Stony Point, and that when Cornwallis gave his sword to the great George, and that when Lee surrendered to Grant, I was there.

I was right in it.

I did it.

I find that I commanded the ships, and sighted the guns, and fired the shells, and stoked the boilers, and managed the engines, at Manila; and at Santiago the same.

It was I who charged up the hill at San Juan, and set the flag a-waving over Ponce.

I am the man that sunk the Merrimac.

I am indispensable and irrepressible.

Nothing can be done in these States and Territories and outlying islands without me.

The millionaire can't get his stuff together in such large piles unless I help him.

He can't build a house, or run a railroad, or open a mine, or start the oil well spouting, or make electric wires talk and work, or turn wool into clothes, or ideas into bank notes, unless I say so.

The missionary can't go unless I send him.

The legislator can't legislate, and magistrate can't enforce the law without my consent.

Not even the Boss can boss things unless I let him.

I'm wonderful.

You can't buy anything unless I sell.

You can't sell anything unless I buy.

You can't teach anything unless I learn.

You can't learn anything unless I teach.

I'm something surprising.

The Greeks and the Romans, and Nebuchadnezzar and Pharaoh and Xerxes never saw anything like me.

I'm English, Irish, French, Spanish, and Portuguese; German, Dutch, Russian, Polish, and Scandinavian; Italian, Greek, and Turk; Chinese, Japanese, and Hawaiian, Australian and Canuck; Afro-American and just plain nigger; cowboy, Indian, Mexicano and a lot more.

❧

I'm simple and I'm complex.
I may not always be right, but I always come right in the end; and I'm pretty certain to get what I want.
I always want something, and generally know exactly what it is.
You never heard of me?
Well, you have.
And you'll hear more of me for a long time to come, for I'm here to stay.
Who am I?
Whoop!
I'm a horny-handed, kid-gloved, knickerbockered, silk-stockinged, swarthy-cheeked, eye-glassed, literary, yellow-journal-reading, church-going, whiskey-drinking, law-abiding, teetotalling, philanthropic, money-grabbing, sentimental, hard-headed, brave, cowardly, independent, boss-ridden, wise, frivolous, hard-working, fun-loving, steady, silly, white-faced, black-faced, copper-colored, well-dressed, unwashed, gentlemanly, rowdyish, all around American Citizen.

"It does sound a *little* like Whitman," I said doubtfully.

"Or take Longfellow's *Excelsior.* Here is my Irish version":

'Twas growing dark so terrible fasht,
When through a town up the mountain there pashed
A broth of a boy, to his neck in the shnow;
As he walked, his shillelagh he swung to and fro,
Saying, "It's till the top I'm bound for to go—
Be jabers!"

I must have dozed briefly at this point. When I opened my eyes, Uncle Allie was still reading:

A bright buxom young girl, such as like to be kissed,

Axed him couldn't he shtop and how could he resist?
So snapping his fingers, and winking his eye,
While smiling upon her he made this reply:
"Faith I meant to kape on till I got to the top,
But as yer swate self has axed me, I may as well shtop—
Be jabers!"

He shtopped all night, and shtopped all day,
And ye mus'n't be axin' whin he did go away,
For wouldn't he be a bastely gossoon
To be lavin his darlint in the swate honeymoon,
Whin the ould man has praties enough and to spare,
Shure he moight as well stay, if he's comfortable there—
Be jabers!

Two more of Uncle Allie's parodies remain in my mind. One was a disrespectful version of "In the Gloaming," a song still popular around the piano in those days:

In the steamer, O my darling! when the foghorns scream and blow,
And the footsteps of the steward softly come and softly go,
When the passengers are groaning with a deep and sincere woe,
Will you think of me and love me, as you did not long ago?

In the cabin, O my darling! think not bitterly of me,
Though I rushed away and left you in the middle of our tea;
I was seized with sudden longing to gaze upon the damp, deep sea—
It was best to leave you then, dear; best for you and best for me.

The second burlesque stemmed from the years he had spent in Scotland:

❧

Lord Lovell stood at his own front door,
Seeking the hole for the key;
His hat was wrecked, and his trousers bore
A rent across either knee,
When down came the beauteous Lady Jane
In fair white draperie.

"Oh, where have you been, Lord Lovell?" she said,
"Oh, where have you been?" said she;
"I have not closed an eye in bed,
And the clock has just struck three.
Who has been standing you on your head
In the ash-barrel, pardie?"

"I am not drunk, Lad' Shane," he said,
"And so late it cannot be;
The clock struck one as I entered—
I heard it two times or three.
It must be the salmon on which I fed
Has been too many for me."

"Go tell your tale, Lord Lovell," she said,
"To the maritime cavalree,
To your grandmother of the hoary head—
To anyone but me;
The door is not used to be opened
With a cigarette for a key."

Mr. Anonymous wrote parodies by the carload. Carping critics might suggest that these substituted for a lack of genuine emotion and creative imagination, forcing him to lean on other men's turns of phrase for his own supreme efforts. They would be wrong. He wrote parodies simply for his own amusement.

At all events, the revelation of his parodic life was the start of a new openness between the two of us. Thenceforward he reminisced to me freely about the experiences that had made him Mr. Anonymous.

9

WHEREIN MR. ANONYMOUS DESCRIBES HIS YOUTH AND MIDDLE YEARS

"You are closed-mouthed, Willard," said Uncle Allie in my junior year. "You learned my true identity when you were five, yet apart from my old friends Idem, Ibid., and Trad., only the three of us here" —Author Unknown whacked his ugly tail on the floor— "know who I am to this day. What I tell you henceforth must likewise remain locked in your heart, for at least as long as I live; and that may be a long time. I embark on my seventieth year next February 22; but I feel like a man in his thirties. I trust I have your promise of silence?"

I nodded.

"Very well, then," said Uncle Allie. "I shall go back to 1879."*

You will recall that I was born in 1860, on a farm near San Francisco. I was the youngest child of an itinerant Baptist preacher, your great-grandfather, a circuit rider known as Bible Richardson. My brothers, sisters, and I received our grounding in English, mathematics, Latin, and Greek at home; our parents could not afford to send us away to school.

Robert Louis Stevenson visited the bay area in 1879, when I was nineteen. Almost at once he fell seriously ill, presumably of the disease that was to carry him off fifteen years later. His physician was my uncle, Dr. William Bamford, the husband of your great-grand-

* The remainder of this chapter brings together anecdotes told by Uncle Allie at intervals over several years. Though the accounts are given in his own words, as best I can recollect them, it is easier for me and I hope clearer for you not to enclose most of them in quotation marks.

mother's sister Cornelia Rand. During the months of Mr. Stevenson's treatment, which as far as I could see consisted of drinking milk and spending as much time as possible in the open, he became a great friend of the Bamfords, and inasmuch as I was a frequent visitor at their home, Mr. Stevenson and I developed a cordial relationship. One day he said to me:

"Alfred, have you decided on your life's work?"

I had to answer that I had not gone past the thought of perhaps scribbling for newspapers and magazines like the rest of the Richardson tribe.

"A worthy ambition," he agreed. "But wouldn't you be a better writer if you knew more of the world than just the bay area of California? Wouldn't it help to start by travelling—perhaps even studying abroad?"

That was all very well, I answered, but impossible. My father had recently died, and the whole burden of keeping my family had fallen on my older brother Dan; I, being now nineteen, was obliged to lend a hand.

"True enough," said Mr. Stevenson. "Still, the time may come when you find yourself abroad. If that happens, you might be willing to do me a favor."

"Gladly," I said; for I had always found him a sweet man.

"First, then, if you ever reach London, please go directly to the lodgings of my good friend William Brighty Rands, and tell him I sent you. He is an estimable gentleman, extremely intelligent—a long, lean fellow—indeed, he looks enough like you to be a cousin." (You must accept my assurance, Willard, that as a young man I was as slender as yourself, and not bad looking, either.) "I am sure he will introduce you to gentlemen and ladies who can help your career.

"Second, I pray you most earnestly to make your way to Edinburgh. I assure you that my parents, out of gratitude for the miracle of new life your uncle has given me, will welcome you as if you were their own son. I even hope you may matriculate at Edinburgh University, as I myself did . . . dear me, dear me, how time flies; it must be ten years ago."

I was tempted, and I took the matter up with Dan. His reaction astonished me.

❧§❧

Why not, he asked, start by panning for gold in the Klondike? Alaska was scarcely a cultural mecca. Yet if I hit pay dirt, the whole Richardson family would benefit; if I failed, I should at least have broadened my own background.

You already know of my Alaskan interlude—the trip north; the cry of "Man overboard!"; the kindness of the fur trappers; my journey across Canada; and my arrival at last in London. My first act after finding a bedsitting room was to present myself at the house of Mr. William Rands. He at once asked me in for tea, over which he cross-examined me for an hour or more about Mr. Stevenson, California, Alaska, my family background, and my plans for the future.

You would have liked Bill Rands, Willard. At the time I met him he was known as the laureate of the nursery. He was especially esteemed for his poems and fairy tales for children—"Lilliput Levee," "Lilliput Legends," and so on. In 1881 he was approaching sixty, about my age when I first met you; but he appeared much younger. He had been a poor man, but finally had attained a decent wage as a reporter in the House of Commons. With the income from his books he was able to live comfortably. Shortly he asked me to share his lodgings, and I accepted.

As Mr. Stevenson had said, there was indeed a physical similarity between Mr. Rands and me, though since his last meeting with R.L.S. he had bloated grossly. In fact I took warning from his obesity, and instituted the series of daily exercises that have enabled me to maintain my present highly creditable figure.*

It turned out that there was an actual, if distant, blood connection between us. My mother—your Great-Grandmother Richardson—was born a Rand, of a family that reached New England in 1635. William was descended from the immigrant Robert Rand's uncle Tom, who for reasons unrecorded added an *s* to the name. After elaborate calculations based on the examinations of many

* Here Uncle Allie performed his famous trick of standing on a six-inch block of wood and touching his palms to the ground without bending his knees.

charts, Bill and I concluded that we were eleventh cousins four times removed.

I must now mention the shock I experienced at my first meeting with Bill Rands's dog.

Mr. Rands, Willard, owned the most grotesque caricature of a dog that has ever offended the human eye—a composite of all the worst features of all the dogs ever bred. I could not dream then that he was to become the best friend I would ever have. Author Unknown, get your lazy belly off the floor and take a bow.

(Author Unknown stretched lazily, let his tongue hang out, and nodded to me, but did not arise. I said, "But that's impossible, Uncle Allie! No dog can be fifty years old!" To which my uncle replied: "Oh, I assure you he is far older than that. His previous owner had willed him to Bill Rands in 1835. When the time comes for you to go through my papers, you will find that Author Unknown has guarded and protected every bearer of the Anonymous name at least since the first Roman invasion of Britain." "What happened when there was more than one Mr. Anonymous at the same time?" I asked. "There is never more than one Mr. Anonymous at the same time," replied Uncle Allie.)

I was astonished (he resumed) to discover that William Rands actually visited the West Coast of the United States in the year 1853. *Harper's Magazine* ran his account of the experience with the foreword, "*The loveliest two weeks we ever heard of were spent by the unknown author of this short piece on a tiny island at Port Orford, Oregon. He was not alone.*" Here are some excerpts from the article:

"It happened thus: A fine clipper ship, which had agreed to carry us around the world, on arriving at San Francisco, consented to prostitute its noble powers to an ignoble office; and instead of visiting the Celestial Regions for teas, sailed to the Chincha Islands for guano, whither I declined going—not being tempted even by the bright eyes and sunny skies of Lima. In consequence I became that most unfortunate of beings, an idler in San Francisco; until one lucky day, when a friend requested me to transact some business for him in Port Orford, Oregon.

English. Why not educate and marry her? She was the daughter of a chief, and her father offered to sell her for a gun and a pair of blankets! To an Indian the word *gun* involves all the happiness attached by us to houses, lands, furniture, books, etc.; therefore the price was not depreciatory of the *article* offered for sale; and considering the scarcity of wives in California and Oregon, and the romance attaching to the act, my lady readers will not be in the least surprised that I should have been tempted to accept the offer. But, on the other hand, a salutary doubt as to the reception my uncivilized bride, although of noble blood, would meet with from the female portion of my family of ignoble blood, decided me to let the forest retain its own, and I declined alliance with the blood of the Tagonishas!

"But the steamer comes in sight. Would you like to see my parting with Graziella? Of course it was touching in the extreme, and my last act was to present her with my red hunting shirt, in virtue of which she now undoubtedly reigns as the belle of Oregon."

Mr. Rands combined two great English puns into an immortal couplet. History is not one of your strong points, Willard, but you may remember that Lord Ellenborough, while Governor-General of India in 1842, contrived the annexation of the city of Scinde. He imparted this triumph to Whitehall by telegraph in one Latin word—*Peccavi*; that is, "I have SINNED." A few years later Governor-General Dalhousie, annexing the territory of Oudh, sought to outdo Ellenborough's wit by transmitting the single word *Vovi*. You look blank, Willard; if you had paid more attention to your Latin and less to Greek sorority girls bearing gifts, you would know that "Vovi" means "I've vowed." It took Bill Rands in his capacity as Anon., however, to combine the two puns into a single verse:

> *Peccavi*, I've Scinde, cried Lord Ellenborough proud;
> Dalhousie, more modest, said *Vovi*, I've Oudh.

I shortly began to make a modest living writing on food and drink, two of my favorite subjects, for the English magazine *Punch*. One example will do for many:

Oh! I have loved thee fondly, ever
  Preferr'd thee to the choicest wine;
From thee my lips they could not sever
  By saying thou contain'dst strychnine.
Did I believe the slander? Never!
  I held thee still to be divine.

For me thy color hath a charm,
  Although' tis true they call thee Pale;
And be thou cold when I am warm,
  As late I've been—so high the scale
Of FAHRENHEIT—and febrile harm
    Allay, refrigerating Ale!

How sweet thou art!—yet bitter, too;
  And sparkling, like satiric fun;
But how much better thee to brew,
  Than a conundrum or a pun,
It is, in every point of view,
  Must be allow'd by every one.

Refresh my heart and cool my throat,
  Light, airy child of malt and hops!
That dost not stuff, engross, and bloat
  The skin, the sides, the chin, the chops,
And burst the buttons off the coat,
  Like stout and porter—fattening slops!

I come now to one of the major sorrows of my life. It would de difficult to describe how close I had come to feel over a few months' time toward Bill Rands—yes, and his dog as well. I could have lived with them happily for the rest of their natural days. It was clear, moreover, that they felt the same sense of affinity for me.

Unfortunately, Bill had a bad habit of standing too close to the edge of the platform of the recently inaugurated London subway trains—tubes, he called them. One day in 1882 a Salvation Army band was playing in the station. The trombonist, pulling back her slide to its ultimate, struck him with her elbow and knocked him off the platform before an oncoming train. By the time the cars stopped, Bill had been separated into several parts.*

I was arguing the scansion of a verse with a *Punch* editor that afternoon, and did not learn of Bill Rands's tragic end for several hours. On receiving the news, I at once rushed home. As the hansom-cab dropped me at our lodgings, I was not surprised to hear issuing from the flat one of the saddest sounds in the world—the howl of a mourning dog. Inside, I found Author Unknown on his haunches, his head lifted, his throat pulsing to produce that ghastly ululation. Yet curiously, as soon as I entered the room, his howling ceased. He raised himself on all fours, and stood studying me, as a man might study some possession for which he had paid a consequential sum. When I walked over to stroke his head, he took my sleeve in his mouth, and led me to the Morris chair that had always been Mr. Rands's favorite. The chair, I gathered, was now mine.

I may commit rhymes, Willard; I may write letters to editors; but I think you know that my deepest feelings are guarded by many locks. At that moment I was still in shock over the loss of my dear friend. In a curious sense, Author Unknown was more practical than I. Before he let me subside into the chair, he insisted on pointing out with his nose a white envelope, superscribed with my name, which lay on the seat. I opened it, and read as follows:

* According to one report, the shocking end to Rands's promising career moved young A. E. Housman so deeply that the future author of "A Shropshire Lad" was unable to speak for several days. Years later, when he finally adverted to the tragic event in a poem, he was still unable to face its full enormity, and deliberately garbled the identity of the protagonists:

> "Hallelujah" was the only observation
> That escaped Lieutenant-Colonel Mary Jane,
> When she tumbled off the platform in the station,
> And was cut in little pieces by the train.
> Mary Jane, the train is through yer:
> Hallelujah, hallelujah!
> We will gather up the fragments that remain.

❧

My dear Alfred:

You may recall a little epitaph I wrote some time ago:

> I suffered so much from printer's errors
> That death for me can hold no terrors;
> I'll bet this stone has been misdated,
> I wish to God I'd been cremated.

I of course was being funny, or thought I was, but just now the verse does not seem to funny any more. Though I write you this letter in the hope that you may not have to read it for many years, the sense is growing on me that I shall not be around much longer.

I have learned to respect as virtually infallible the insights of my dog, some day to be yours, Author Unknown. Recently I have felt in him the solicitude of one anticipating the loss of an infinitely dear friend. I have seen him also studying you, as a slave studies a new master; for if some unforeseen event should take me from you, his master you will be perforce.

If the worst happens, Author Unknown will see to it that you receive this letter.

You belong, Alfred, to an everyday family. It carries, however, a recessive gene that regularly becomes dominant in one member of the family: the gene of ANONYMOUS.

ANONYMOUS is driven to express himself without credit, in verse or prose. Since the mantle fell on me, I have even found myself scribbling verses on my detachable cuffs. Each Anonymous is made aware of his heir in due course; and since your arrival in London, I have known that you are destined to succeed me.

I do not tell you this to place an obligation upon you. The obligation is already built into your genes. As the present Mr. Anonymous, let me say only that I have loved you; that I transmit my commitment to you with confidence; and that if ever you are uncertain of your path, Author Unknown will show you the way.

Your affectionate cousin,
William Rands

I found that Mr. Rands had left me enough in consols to live modestly without fear of debtor's prison. One of my first acts was to take the train north, as Mr. Stevenson had urged me, to Edinburgh. There Mr. and Mrs. Thomas Stevenson welcomed me kindly, as he had promised. I stayed in Edinburgh for four years, attended the University, and took a first in Latin and Gaelic. At Edinburgh I brought to perfection that great old Scottish song:

O ye'll tak' the high road, and I'll tak' the low road,
And I'll be in Scotland afore ye;
But me and my true love will never meet again,
On the bonnie, bonnie banks o' Loch Lomon'.

Mine is the credit, too, for the ballad that begins:

Woo'd and married and a',
Woo'd and married and a'
Was she nae very weel aff,
Woo'd and married and a'.

After completing my studies at Edinburgh I crossed the water to Ireland, where I am still remembered for such expressions as

Corn beef and cabbage
Make the Irish savage

and "An Irishman is never at peace except when he's fighting."

I suspect my paean to the Irish potato, or spud, has never been equalled:

Sublime potatoes! that, from Antrim's shore
To famous Kerry, form the poor man's store;

Agreeing well with every place and state—
The peasant's noggin, or the rich man's plate.
Much prized when smoking from the teeming pot,
Or in turf embers roasted crisp and hot.
Welcome, although you be our only dish;
Welcome, companion to flesh, fowl, or fish;
But to the real gourmands, the learned few,
Most welcome, steaming in an Irish stew.

To change the subject for a moment, Willard, you may have wondered—indeed, I have asked myself—how it happened that I never married. My interest in the opposite sex is self-evident. But the nature of the bargain I accepted in becoming Mr. Anonymous—and it was accepted freely—requires long periods of solitude and a heavy injection of self-centeredness. It requires also, if I may so put it, a generalization rather than specification of desire; all women interest me more than any one of them does. And to be frank, women frighten me a little.

During my first years as Mr. Anonymous, I often dreamed of throwing myself at the feet of some appreciative female. I did not care whether she was tall or tiny, tawny or rufous, partridge-plump or pin-thin. My only criterion was that she must be aware of the ridiculous. But the question immediately ensued: if indeed she was aware of the ridiculous, would not my throwing myself at her feet, doubtless ardently embracing her knees as well, activate her risibilities? And if she laughed at me, would I not withdraw humiliated into my carapace? If she did not laugh, would I not wonder for the rest of my life whether she had restrained herself solely to spare my feelings? In those days women kept their sense of the absurd well hidden. Indeed, I can recall only one who let it into the open—a Mrs. Edward Craster, whose remarks on the centipede have found a permanent home in *Bartlett's Quotations*. I might have approached Mrs. Craster with romantic intent; but she was already married.

Do you suppose that in Victorian days little girls' nursemaids placed a taboo on the ridiculous, even before the girls had learned to write their names? When J. Parton wrote "The Humorous Poetry of the English Language" in 1856, he commented in his preface:

> An unexpected feature of [this] book is that there is not a line in it by a female hand. The alleged foibles of the Fair have given occasion to libraries of comic verse; yet, with diligent search, no humorous poems by women have been found which are of merit sufficient to give them claim to a place in a collection like this. That lively wit and graceful gayety, that quick perception of the absurd, which ladies are continually displaying in their conversation and correspondence, never, it seems, suggest the successful epigram, or inspire happy satirical verse.

What a contrast with the first half of the following century, glittering like a Christmas tree with the likes of Carolyn Wells, Dorothy Parker, and Phyllis McGinley!

But to return to marriage: though many married men have been invested over the generations with the Anonymous mantle, I know of none who married *after* he became Mr. Anonymous. I have no idea of the reason for this, nor why to the best of my knowledge there has never been a *Miss* Anonymous. I recall one Christmas in the nineties when, almost tempted into a proposal by a lass with an irresistible Scottish brogue, I was saved from domesticity only by concentrating on an unusually heavy dinner. I wrote next day:

It may not be—go maidens, go,
Nor tempt me to the mistletoe;
I once could dance beneath its bough,
But must not, will not, can not, now!

A weight—a load within I bear;
It is not madness nor despair;
But I require to be at rest,
So that my burden may digest.

I have no idea whether I wrote the following verse out of bitter experience or simply to pun:

To win the maid the poet tries,
And sometimes writes to Julia's eyes;—
She *likes* a verse—but, cruel whim,
She still appears *a-verse* to him.

The punning explanation seems the more likely. The only love verse of mine that I can swear sprang from the heart was written while I was still attending Edinburgh University. You may think that institutions of higher learning were confined to the male of the species in those days, but not so; there was a scattering of the opposite sex, one of whom, in my chemistry class, all but drove me to such a clap of thunder as water produces on sodium. Here are the first lines of a long poem I wrote to her:

I love thee, Mary, and thou lovest me—
Our mutual flame is like th' affinity
That doth exist between two simple bodies:
I am Potassium to thine Oxygen.
'Tis little that the holy marriage vow
Shall shortly make us one. That unity
Is, after all, but metaphysical.
O, would that I, my Mary, were an acid;
A living acid; thou an alkali
Endow'd with human sense, that, brought together,
We might both coalesce into one salt,
One homogeneous crystal. Oh! that thou
Were Carbon, and myself were Hydrogen;
We would unite to form olefiant gas,
Or common coal, or naphtha—would to heaven
That I were Phosphorus, and thou wert Lime!
And we of Lime composed a Phosphuret.
I'd be content to be Sulphuric Acid,
So that thou might be Soda. In that case
We would be Glauber's Salt. Wert thou Magnesia
Instead we'd form the salt that's named from Epsom.
Couldst thou Potassa be, I Aqua-fortis,
Our happy union should that compound form,
Nitrate of Potash—otherwise Saltpetre.
And thus our several natures sweetly blent,
We'd live and love together, until death
Should decompose the fleshly *tertium quid*,
Leaving our souls to all eternity
Amalgamated . . .

If memory serves, our mutual attentions ended when the first clap of thunder turned to a thunderous clap.

The girls of the town interested me more than those of the drawing room. I regarded the marital state with neurotic suspicion:

Which is of greater value, prythee, say,
  The Bride or Bridegroom?—Must the truth be
    told?
Alas, it must! The bride is given away—
  The bridegroom's often regularly sold.

Indeed, the only marriage I would even have considered was of the sort described in this appeal to a rich young widow:

I will not ask if you canst touch
  The tuneful ivory key;
Those silent notes of yours are such
  As quite suffice for me.

I'll make no question of thy skill
  The pencil comprehends,
Enough for me, love, if thou still
  Canst draw thy dividends!

Without some such inducement, I saw marriage as one long quarrel, not so much between husband and wife as between them and their creditors:

O fling not this receipt away,
  Given by one who trusted thee;
Mistakes will happen every day
  However honest folks may be.
And sad it is, love, twice to pay;
  So cast not that receipt away!

Ah, yes; if e'er, in future hours,
  When we this bill have all forgot,
They send it in again—ye powers!—
  And swear that we have paid it not—
How sweet to know, on such a day
  We've never cast receipts away!

10

WHEREIN MR. ANONYMOUS TAKES HIS LEAVE—OR DOES HE?

Uncle Alfred was more reticent about the next ten or fifteen years, when his fancy seems to have been diverted from verse to the art of photography. On a weekend visit at the home of the mathematician Charles Lutwidge Dodgson, Uncle Allie was greatly taken with Dodgson's experiments in this medium. Returning shortly thereafter to the United States he photographed many still-wild territories before settling into an academic career. He frequented ranches, mountains, forests, and gold mines. There remains from this period a hodgepodge of yellowing photographs and little-known cattle songs and folk ballads. One will give the general tenor:

Song of the Cattle Trail

The dust hangs thick upon the trail
And the horns and the hoofs are clashing,
While off at the side through the chapparal
The men and the strays go crashing;
But in right good cheer the cowboy sings,
For the work of the fall is ending,
And then it's ride for the old home ranch,
Where a maid love's light is tending.

Then it's crack! crack! crack!
On the beef steer's back,
And it's run, you slow-foot devil;
For I'm soon to turn back where through the black
Love's lamp gleams along the level . . .

Then it's quirt! quirt! quirt!
And it's run or git hurt,
You hang-back, bawling critter.
For a man who's in love with a turtle dove
Ain't got no time to fritter.

I was graduated from Redlands in 1930 and left at once for France to study philosophy and girls at the Sorbonne. I remember that as the train began to move, Uncle Allie bounded along the platform, Author Unknown beside him. Uncle Allie was singing in falsetto,

Passengers will please refrain
From flushing toilets while the train
Is in the station tell me that you love me . . .

I lost the rest of the song; the train was picking up speed, and he fell behind. For the next few years Uncle Allie and I saw each other only intermittently. In 1932, I settled in New York City, where I still live. In the early thirties, my greatest ambition was to have the columnist F. P. A. print a poem of mine in *The Conning Tower.* I tried and tried, but as far as my files show he used only two. I kept the clippings; they were important to me then:

Shadow Song

Pity, pity, pity
How the cypress spread;
Softly sing your ditty,
Soon the quick are dead.

Tiptoe, tiptoe lightly,
Lest you wake one sleeping;
Whisper whitely, whitely,
Lest you set one weeping.

Softly touch the clay,
It is fragile stuff;
Hurt it not, decay
Cometh prompt enough.

Softly, softly sing to
Heartbeats hiding woe;
Haste them tunes to cling to,
Even now they slow.

Fleetly, fleetly, fleetly,
Minutes may not stay;
Let a song go sweetly
When you go away.

Reddened Roses

Flowers to dizen my darling;
Wreaths for her head;
My lovely is loath of white roses?
Grow her red.

Pout not, my patienceless pretty;
Droop not, my doe;
I forest my heart with red roses;
They grow slow.

My dear has forsaken my garden;
My fair one has fled;
I wheedled my sweet with white roses
Painted red.

Passed here a maiden, of sorrow
Stilly aflood,
Fine at the throat with a dead bouquet
Bathed in blood?

I know I was driving at something in those two poems. But I have no idea what it was.

The years passed. I worked on magazines and wrote advertising and public relations copy. Mr. Anonymous remained at Redlands. We corresponded occasionally, generally when one or the other of us had something in print that he wanted to show off. Once Uncle Allie sent me a typed clerihew that he apparently thought too unkind to publish:

❧

Miss Katherine Anne Porter
Writes worse than she orter
Her efforts are uppity
And not my cuppity.

In 1940, Mr. Anonymous, then eighty years old, was reluctantly permitted by his superiors at the University of Redlands to retire. He and Author Unknown removed to his earlier quarters in Oysterville. He swiftly transformed the cottage into the same dump heap of books, papers, and cardboard boxes it had been nearly a quarter of a century before. I visited him there, usually once or twice a year. Our reunions were always joyous, often ribald, and sometimes drunken. In fact, I had begun to take on certain of his characteristics. I had grown considerably heavier; and I must say that on me the extra weight sat very well.

The mind of Mr. Anonymous remained keen; but he sometimes would doze off in the middle of a sentence. The nap would continue for as many as fifteen minutes, while Author Unknown lay with chin on paws, eyes fixed unblinkingly on his master, his horrible Pekinese features a caricature of adoration. When Uncle Allie woke he would pick up his sentence in midair and continue as if there had been no interruption.

I did notice a softening process in his views. Cynical remarks grew rarer; he was more likely to revert to sentimental observations recorded in his earlier life. The last poem he ever read to me was written, I imagine, not by him but by some earlier Mr. Anonymous:

I know where I'm going.
I know who's going with me,
I know who I love,
But the dear knows who I'll marry.

I'll have stockings of silk,
Shoes of fine green leather,
Combs to buckle my braid,
And a ring for every finger.

Feather beds are soft,
Painted rooms are bonny;
But I'd leave them all
To go with my love Johnny.

Some say he's dark,
I say he's bonny,
He's the flower of them all,
My handsome, coaxing Johnny.

I know where I'm going.
I know who's going with me,
I know who I love,
But the dear knows who I'll marry.

He read that, then looked sheepish, and remarked, half-smiling, shuffling his feet like an embarrassed schoolboy:

"I am pleased that you did not remain a bachelor, Willard. I have always underestimated women. I should have listened to them, I should have listened. They have much to teach."

We said our last good bye in the summer of 1976. A few months later, glancing through my morning mail, I found an envelope addressed to me in a shaky, spidery hand that had become as familiar to me as my own. The letter read:

My dear boy:

Boy no more, I suppose, for it must be close to sixty years since I first found you digging in your sandpile. It is hard to count straight these days, but if the family Bible is correct, I am nearing 116, which for a Richardson is unprecedented, and even for Mr. Anonymous is getting along. I cannot expect to last much longer. I have nothing to leave you except the papers you know about and such attitudes as I may have planted, or at least manured, in your subconscious. You may think the sentimental enclosure proof that I have entered my dotage; the man who wrote it would have been, in the Anonymous line, my great-great-grandfather. (I remind myself of a friend you once mentioned who, dying, remarked that in his healthy years he had not believed in an afterlife. He said that now he did believe—but only in heaven, not in hell.)

It is unlikely that I shall see you again. I think I need not tell you the comfort you have been to me. No paralepsis between us, my boy! Live well, live long; live while you live. So nothing more, for now, from your loving

Uncle Allie

The enclosure read as follows:

Paper found in Old Saint Paul's Church, Baltimore, Maryland, dated 1692, unattributed:

Go placidly amid the noise and the haste, and remember what peace there may be in silence. As far as possible without surrender, be on good terms with all persons. Speak your truth quietly and clearly; and listen to others, even the dull and ignorant; they too have their story. Avoid loud and aggressive persons, they are vexations to the spirit. If you compare yourself with others you may become vain and bitter; for always there will be greater and lesser persons than yourself.

Enjoy your achievements as well as your plans. Keep interested in your own career, however humble; it is a real possession in the changing fortunes of time. Exercise caution in your business affairs; for the world is full of trickery. But let this not blind you to what virtue there is; many persons strive for high ideals; and everywhere life is full of heroism. Be yourself. Especially do not feign affection. Neither be cynical about love; for in the face of all aridity and disenchantment it is as perennial as the grass.

Take kindly the counsel of the years, gracefully surrendering the things of youth. Nurture strength of spirit to shield you in sudden misfortune. But do not distress yourself with imaginings. Many fears are born of fatigue and loneliness. Beyond a wholesome discipline, be gentle with yourself. You are a child of the universe no less than the trees and the stars; you have a right to be here. And whether or not it is clear to you, no doubt the universe is unfolding as it should.

Therefore be at peace with God, whatever you conceive Him to be; and whatever your labors and aspirations, in the noisy confusion of life keep peace with your soul. With all its sham, drudgery and broken dreams, it is still a beautiful world. Be careful. Strive to be happy.

There was a P.S.:

I add these lines to prove I am not a complete sentimentalist, even now:

> Hey nonny no!
> Men are fools that wish to die!
> Is't not fine to dance and sing
> When the bells of death do ring?
> Is't not fine to swim in wine
> And turn upon the toe
> And sing hey nonny no,
> When the winds blow and the seas flow?
> Hey nonny no!

I cancelled my appointments and took the next available non-stop flight for the West Coast.

At Oysterville, I went directly to Uncle Allie's. He was sitting in an old chair, a blanket over his knees, dozing; the cottage was very hot; a fire was roaring up the flue, and I wondered who had been piling on the logs. Author Unknown lay as always at his master's feet. I did not wake the old man but sat looking at him, remembering. At last he opened his bulbous eyes, became aware of my presence, and nodded in quiet satisfaction. "Ah, there you are," he said, his squeak a little tremulous. "You shouldn't have come, of course, but I knew you would." His head drooped again. I thought he was dozing until he said, pausing between the words, "I think everything is settled between us, my boy, except for one thing. I have never spoken to you about Author Unknown. Someone is going to have to care for him after I am gone, and I had been hoping it would be you."

"Of course I will take him, Uncle Allie. If you are sure I am the right one."

"Ah yes," he said, his fingers fumbling with a book on his lap, "for sixty years now I have known you were the right one." The book slipped through his fingers and fell to the floor; his head drooped lower. Author Unknown leaped suddenly to his feet, the hairs on his bony back erect. A low growl, or maybe it was a sob, issued from his throat. Then he threw back his head, and howled.

I sat for a long while, unwilling to accept life with no Mr. Anonymous. I looked at him, sitting there as if asleep, and wondered: what will the world do now, with no one left to print the truths that no one dares print under his own name? The nearest thing to a tear I had managed in half a century worked its way from the corner of my eye and dribbled along my cheek like a creek sinking into dry soil.

The next thing I remember, Author Unknown, using paw and nose, was pushing across the floor toward me the book that had dropped from Uncle Allie's lap. Author Unknown never acted without a reason; I picked up the volume, a paperback from a little-known press. The dog laid his chin on my knee and watched as I riffled through the pages. A line struck a chord in my memory. One line —two—half a dozen. I read them for the first time in forty-eight years, while the smoke swirled up once more from some internal pentagon:

> Seek not beauty; seek not wit;
> Seek not wealth, or but a bit.
> Seek instead the maiden who
> Seeks no other man but you.
> She will be when you are gone
> Loyalty's own paragon;

She her virtue well will shield,
And, when she cannot but yield,
For one moment, maybe two,
May pretend that He is You.

—*Anonymous*

The womb's a fine and private place
In which to propagate the race.

—*Anonymous*

PART II

SELECTED WORKS OF THE ANONYMOUS CLAN

Uncle Allie had never been a systematic man. The Winslow cottage (which I am now in the process of turning into a hideaway-study for my own scribbling) is still jammed with his crates and cardboard boxes. I have pried off the tops of the crates with hammer-claws, and cut with shears the cords that held together dissolving cardboard containers. But when I began the process of organizing the manuscripts he had squirreled away over a century, I was at a loss. The dampness of Oysterville had turned much of the paper back into pulp. Older, tougher material was often covered with faded script in languages and even alphabets that baffled me. I needed help and found it in a distant relative on the Rand side—Lester Eldridge, a young assistant to the President of Evergreen College in Olympia. Lester provided student help in analyzing and arranging this detritus. Even so, the process will take a long time. I shall not be surprised if it turns out that some of the parchments are as old as the Tutankhamun's tomb.

It is my hope that all the writings saved by Uncle Allie will be included in my pending *Encyclopedia Anonymica*, conceived as an organized summary of literature handed down by the Anonymous clan since the day man first began to write. Such a definitive compilation, however, is long in the future. Meanwhile, I hope you will find pleasure in the following sampling of verses written either by Uncle Allie or his predecessors.

From a collection including no less than 10,000 verses, perhaps twice that many, how can I choose those that best evoke Mr. Anonymous? There is no way. If I quoted only his most familiar lines, I would simply be repeating what you already know. If I eliminated everything you know, his greatness would be lost. If I concentrated on any one category—parodies, limericks, or whatever—I would bore you. So I will give you a little of this and a little of that, and hope you leave the table wanting more.

ADVERTISING

As best I can reconstruct the events of Mr. Anonymous's life, he at no time worked as a salaried employee for an advertising agency. He frequently, however, submitted slogans that became the basis of notable advertising campaigns. Among these, besides those mentioned earlier, are "Save the Surface and you Save all" (for Sherwin-Williams Paint); "His Master's Voice" (for Victrola); and "Hasn't scratched yet" (for Bon Ami).

ON ALCOHOL

Mr. A. had a tendency to confuse love with liquor; when tiddly he often fancied himself in love, and when in love he often became tiddly. He might well have said, if he did not, "I could not love thee, dear, so much, loved I not whiskey more."

God, in His Goodness

God, in his goodness, sent the grape
To cheer both great and small;
Little fools will drink too much
And great fools none at all.

Once, Twice, Thrice

Once, twice, thrice, I Julia tried,
The scornful puss as oft denied,
And since I can no longer thrive,
I'll cringe to never a bitch alive.
So kiss my Arse, disdainful sow!
Good claret is my mistress now.

Love

There's the wonderful love of a beautiful maid,
And the love of a staunch true man,
And the love of a baby that's unafraid—
All have existed since time began.

But the most wonderful love, the Love of all loves,
Even greater than the love for Mother,
Is the infinite, tenderest, passionate love
Of one dead drunk for another.

ON ANIMALS

Mr. Anonymous considered animals his equal, if not his superiors. Cat, dog, goose, ox, horse, turtle, crocodile, whatever—they all received from him the same courteous respect he accorded a beautiful woman. When he reported an encounter between a boy and a crocodile (see page 15), his sympathies clearly lay with the animal, not the human. The only unkind word he ever wrote about an animal was in a takeoff on a Thomas Moore poem, which I include to balance his general anthropomorphism.

'Twas Ever Thus
(AFTER THOMAS MOORE)

I never bought a young gazelle,
  To glad me with its soft black eye,
But, when it came to know me well,
  'Twas sure to butt me on the sly.

I never drilled a cockatoo,
  To speak with almost human lip,
But, when a pretty phrase it knew,
  'Twas sure to give some friend a nip.

I never trained a collie hound
  To be affectionate and mild,
But, when I thought a prize I'd found
  'Twas sure to bite my youngest child.

I never kept a tabby kit
  To cheer my leisure with its tricks,
But, when we'd all grew fond of it,
  'Twas sure to catch the neighbor's chicks.

I never reared a turtle-dove,
  To coo all day with gentle breath,

But, when its life seemed one of love,
'Twas sure to peck its mate to death.

I never—well I never yet—
And I have spent no end of pelf—
Invested money in a pet
That didn't misconduct itself.

Lines by a Humanitarian

Be lenient with lobsters, and ever kind to crabs,
And be not disrespectful to cuttle-fish or dabs;
Chase not the Cochin-China, chaff not the ox obese,
And babble not of feather-beds in company with geese.
Be tender with the tadpole, and let the limpet thrive,
Be merciful to mussels, don't skin your eels alive;
When talking to a turtle don't mention callipee—
Be always kind to animals wherever you may be.

Ode to a Bobtailed Cat

Felix Infelix! Cat unfortunate,
With nary narrative!
Canst thou no tail relate
Of how
(Miaow!)
Thy tail end came to terminate so bluntly
Didst wear it off be
Sedentary habits
As do the rabbits?

Didst go a
Fishing with it
Wishing it
To "bob" for catfish,
And get bobbed thyself?
Curses on that fish!

Didst lose it in kittenhood,
Hungrily chawing it?
Or, gaily pursuing it,
Did it make tangent
From thy swift circuit?

Did some brother greyback—
Yowling
And howling
In nocturnal strife,
Spitting and staring
Cursing and swearing,
Ripping and tearing,
Calling thee "Sausagetail,"
Abbreviate thy suffix?

Or did thy jealous wife
Detect yer
In some sly flirtation,
And, after caudal lecture,
Bite off thy termination?
And sarve yar right!

Did some mischievous boy,
Some barbarous boy,
Eliminate thy finis?
(Probably!)
The wretch!
The villain!

Cruelly spillin'
Thy innocent blood!
Furiously scratch him
Where'er yer may catch him!

Well, Bob, this course now is left,
Since thus of your tail you're bereft;
Tell your friend that by letter
From Paris
You have learned the style there is
To wear the tail short
And the briefer the better;
Such is the passion,
That every Grimalkin will
Follow your fashion.

A Cat's Conscience

A dog will often steal a bone,
But conscience lets him not alone,
And by his tail his guilt is known.

But cats consider theft a game,
And, howsoever you may blame,
Refuse the slightest sign of shame.
When food mysteriously goes,
That chances are that Pussy knows
More than she leads you to suppose.

And hence there is no need for you,
If Puss declines a meal or two,
To feel her pulse and make ado.

The Kilkenny Cats

There wanst was two cats at Kilkenny,
Each thought there was one cat too many,
So they quarrell'd and fit,
They scratch'd and they bit,
Till, excepting their nails,
And the tips of their tails,
Instead of two cats, there warn't any.

The Canny Crocodile

There once was a crocodile, old and stout,
And a trifle clumsy at getting about;
He was chiefly found in the River Nile—
This lumbersome, cumbersome crocodile.

Sometimes all day on the sand he'd lie,
And deeply and thoughtfully wonder why.
Then he'd smile a slow, inscrutable smile—
This emotional, notional crocodile.

If a friend came by for a cosy chat,
He would noisily argue on this or that.

His opponent's opinions he would revile—
This babbling, scrabbling crocodile.

Sometimes he would stand up on the shore,
And declaim in a voice like the ocean's roar.
His sonorous speech could be heard a mile—
This wonderful, thunderful crocodile.

You see, by his crafty and subtle art,
He made people believe he was clever and smart.
They praised his wisdom, his speech, his style—
This notable, quotable crocodile!

Kindly Advice

Be kind to the panther! for when thou wert young,
 In thy country far over the sea,
'Twas a panther ate up thy papa and mama,
 And had several mouthfuls of thee!

Be kind to the badger! for who shall decide
 The depth of his badgery soul?
And think of the tapir, when flashes the lamp
 O'er the fast and the free flowing bowl.

Be kind to the camel! nor let word of thine
 Ever put up his bactrian back;
And cherish the she-kangeroo with her bag,
 Nor venture to give her the sack.

Be kind to the ostrich! For how canst thou hope
 To have such a stomach as it?
And when the proud day of your "bridal" shall come,
 Do give the poor birdie a "bit."

Be kind to the walrus! nor ever forget
 To have it on Tuesday to tea;
But butter the crumpets on only one side,
 Save such as are eaten by thee.

Be kind to the bison! and let the jackal
 In the light of thy love have a share;
And coax the ichneumon to grow a new tail,
 And have lots of larks in its lair!

Be kind to the bustard, that genial bird,
  And humor its wishes and ways;
And when the poor elephant suffers from bile,
  Then tenderly lace up his stays!

The Common Cormorant or Shag

The common cormorant or shag
Lays eggs inside a paper bag.
The reason you will see no doubt—
It is to keep the lightning out.
But what these unobservant birds
Have never noticed is that herds
Of wandering bears may come with buns
And steal the bags to hold the crumbs.

FOR CHILDREN

Uncle Allie loved children almost as much as he loved animals, women, and strong spirits. Such philoprogenitiveness is a characteristic of the Anonymous tribe, for whom, however, it tends to be a spectator rather than a participatory sport. Perhaps they idealized children because so few of the clan ever married and had children of their own. It is sometimes hard to tell whether Uncle Allie was aiming a verse at an audience of children, or simply writing childishly. The nursery rhymes of his forebears—rhymes that have changed the soul of our language—were often written, I should guess, with a highly adult concept in mind.

Animal Fair

I went to the animal fair,
The birds and beasts were there.
The big baboon, by the light of the moon,
Was combing his auburn hair.
The monkey, he got drunk,
And sat on the elephant's trunk.
The elephant sneezed and fell on his knees,
And what became of the monk, the monk?

A Pleasant Ship

I saw a ship a-sailing,
A-sailing on the sea,
And oh! it was laden
With pretty things for thee!

There were comfits in the cabin,
And apples in the hold;
The sails were made of silk,
And the masts were made of gold.

The four-and-twenty sailors
That stood between the decks
Were four-and-twenty white mice,
With chains about their necks.

The captain was a duck,
With a packet on his back,
And when the ship began to move,
The captain said "Quack! Quack!"

Three young rats with black felt hats,
Three young ducks with white straw flats,
Three young dogs with curling tails,
Three young cats with demi-veils,
Went out to walk with two young pigs
In satin vests and sorrel wigs;
But suddenly it chanced to rain,
And so they all went home again.

I Had a Little Nut-Tree

I had a little nut-tree, nothing would it bear
But a golden nutmeg and a silver pear;
The King of Spain's daughter came to visit me
And all for the sake of my little nut-tree.
I skipped over water, I danced over sea,
And all the birds in the air couldn't catch me.

EPITAPHS

Mr. Anonymous was almost as touchy about epitaphs as he was about limericks, and admitted to authorship of only a fraction of those attributed to him. The last of those that follow is the work of his immediate predecessor. The rest are his own.

On Uncle Peter Dan'els

Beneath this stone, a lump of clay,
  Lies Uncle Peter Dan'els,
Who, early in the month of May,
  Took off his winter flannels.

To the Four Husbands of Miss Ivy Saunders
1790, 1794, 1808, 18—?

Here lie my husbands One Two Three
  Dumb as men could ever be
As for my fourth well praise be God
  He bides a little above the sod
Alex Ben Sandy were the
  First three names
And to make things tidy
  I'll add his—James

On Mary Ann Lowder

Here lies the body of Mary Ann Lowder,
She burst while drinking a seidlitz powder.
Called from this world to her heavenly rest,
She should have waited till it effervesced.

On Moll Batchelor

Beneath in the Dust, the mouldy old Crust
Of *Moll Batchelor* lately was shoven,
Who was skill'd in the Arts of Pyes, Custards and Tarts,
And every Device of the Oven.
When she'd liv'd long enough, she made her last Puff,
A Puff by her Husband much prais'd;
And here she doth lie, and makes a Dirt Pye,
In Hopes that her Crust may be rais'd.

Johnny Dow

Wha lies here?
I, Johnny Dow.
Hoo! Johnny is that you?
Ay, man, but a'm dead now.

On John Grubb

When from the chrysalis of the tomb,
I rise in rainbow-coloured plume,
My weeping friends, ye scarce will know
That I was but a Grubb below.

On My Gude Auntie

Here lies my gude and gracious Auntie
Whom Death has packed in his portmanty.

Epitaph from Aberdeen

Here lie the bones of Elizabeth Charlotte
Born a virgin, died a harlot
She was aye a virgin at seventeen
A remarkable thing in Aberdeen.

Gaily I lived as ease and nature taught,
And spent my little life without a thought;
And am annoyed that Death, that tyrant grim,
Should think of me, who never thought of him.

From a Tombstone to a Fish That Lived for Twenty Years, in the Village of Blockley, Gloucestershire:

Under the soil the old fish do lie 20 year he lived and then did die He was so tame you understand He would come and eat out of your hand Died April the 20th 1855.

Epitaph on a Marf

Wot a marf 'e'd got,
Wot a marf.
When 'e was a kid,
Goo' Lor' lov'll
'Is pore old muvver
Must 'a' fed 'im wiv a shuvvle.

Wot a gap 'e'd got,
Pore Chap,
'E'd never been known to larf,
'Cos if 'e did
It's a penny to a quid
'E'd 'a' split 'is fice in 'arf.

Epitaph on a Geologist

Where shall we our great professor inter
  That in peace he may rest his bones?
If we hew him a rocky sepulchre,
  He'll rise and break the stones,

And examine each stratum that lies around,
For he's quite in his element under ground.

If with mattock and spade his body we lay
In the common alluvial soil,
He'll start up and snatch those tools away,
Of his own geological toil;
In a stratum so young the professor disdains
That imbedded should be his organic remains.

Thus expos'd to the drop of some case hard'ning spring
His carcase let stalactite cover;
And to Oxford the petrified sage let us bring,
When he is encrusted all over;
Then 'mid mammoths and crocodiles, high on a shelf,
Let him stand as a monument rais'd to himself.

ON FOOD

Mr. Anonymous was a trencherman who would have staggered Falstaff or Tom Jones. His ideal benediction at dinner was

Heavenly father bless us,
And keep us all alive;
There's ten of us for dinner
And not enough for five.

His verse recipes, long a feature of *Punch*, made many laugh, but he was perfectly serious about them; from a stack as high as my head, I have chosen three to give you the idea. Also included is a Roast Swan song which might better have gone under Animals.

Get Up, Get Up

Get up, get up, you lazy-head,
  Get up you lazy sinner,
We need those sheets for tablecloths,
  It's nearly time for dinner!

Roast Swan Song

Aforetime, by the waters wan,
This lovely body I put on:
In life I was a stately swan.

  Ah me! Ah me!
Now browned and basted thoroughly.

Once I was whiter than the snow,
The fairest bird that earth could show;
Now I am blacker than the crow.

  Ah me! Ah me!

Would I might glide, my fluffing,
On pools to feel the cool wind soughing,
Rather than burst with pepper-stuffing.

Ah me! Ah me!

The cook now turns me round and turns me.
The hurrying waiter next concerns me,
But oh, this fire, how sore it burns me!

Ah me! Ah me!

Here I am dished upon the platter.
I cannot fly. Oh, what's the matter?
Lights flash, teeth clash—I fear the latter.

Ouch! . . . Ouch! . . .

Barley Broth

A basin of barley broth make, make for me;
Give those who prefer it, the plain:
No matter of broth, so of barley it be,
If we ne'er taste a basin again.
For, oh! when three pounds of good mutton you buy,
And of most of its fat dispossess it,
In a stewpan uncover'd, at first, let it lie;
Then in water proceed to dress it.
Hurrah! hurrah! hurrah!
In a stewpan uncover'd, at first let it lie;
Then in water proceed to dress it.

What a teacup will hold—you should first have been told—
Of barley you gently should boil;
The pearl-barley choose—'tis the nicest that's sold—
All others the mixture might spoil.
Of carrots and turnips, small onions, green peas
(If the price of the last don't distress one),
Mix plenty; and boil all together with these
Your basin of broth when you dress one.
Hurrah! hurrah! hurrah!
Two hours together the articles boil;
There's your basin of broth, if you'd dress one.

The Christmas Pudding

If you wish to make a pudding in which everyone delights,
Of a dozen new-laid eggs you must take the yolks and whites;
Beat them well up in a basin till they thoroughly combine,
And shred and chop some suet particularly fine;

Take a pound of well-stoned raisins, and a pound of currants dried,
A pound of pounded sugar, and a pound of peel beside;
Stir them all well up together with a pound of wheaten flour,
And let them stand and settle for a quarter of an hour;

Then tie the pudding in a cloth, and put it in the pot—
Some people like the water cold, and some prefer it hot;
But though I don't know which of these two methods I should praise,
I know it ought to boil an hour for every pound it weighs.

Oh! if I were Queen of France, or, still better, Pope of Rome,
I'd have a Christmas pudding every day I dined at home;
And as for other puddings whatever they might be,
Why those who like the nasty things should eat them all for me.

Homoeopathic Soup

Take a robin's leg
(Mind, the drumstick merely);
Put it in a tub
Filled with water nearly;
Set it out of doors
In a place that's shady;
Let it stand a week
(Three days if for a lady);
Drop a spoonful of it
In a five-pail kettle,
Which may be made of tin

Or any baser metal;
  Fill the kettle up,
Set it on a boiling,
  Strain the liquor well,
To prevent its oiling;
  One atom add of salt,
For the thickening one rice kernel,
  And use to light the fire
  "The Homoeopathic Journal."
  Let the liquor boil
Half an hour, no longer,
  (If 'tis for a man
Of course you'll make it stronger).
  Should you now desire
That the soup be flavoury,
  Stir it once around
With a stalk of savoury.
  When the broth is made,
Nothing can excell it:
  Then three times a day
Let the patient *smell* it.
  If he chance to die,
Say 'twas Nature did it;
  If he chance to live,
Give the soup the credit.

FUN

It may bother you, and you may be right in being bothered, that Uncle Allie left no profound message behind him. Precisely because he realized the ultimate sadness of life, he lived for fun, and he wrote for fun. I cannot say I am a better man for having read the following verses. All I can say is that I enjoyed them.

'Bon soir, ma chérie,
Comment allez-vous?'
'Je suis très bien,
Merci beaucoup.'

'Etes-vous fiancé?'
'San fairy-ann.'
'Voulez-vous promenader avec moi ce soir?'

'Oui, oui—'
'Combien?'

We Be Soldiers Three

We be soldiers three,
Pardonnez-moi je vous en prie,
Lately come forth of the low country,
With never a penny of money.
Here, good fellow, I drink to thee,
Pardonnez-moi je vous en prie,
To all good fellows wherever they be,
With never a penny of money.
And he that will not pledge me this,
Pardonnez-moi je vous en prie,
Pays for the shot, whatever it is,
With never a penny of money.
Charge it again, boys, charge it again,
Pardonnez-moi je vous en prie,
As long as you have any ink in your pen,
With never a penny of money.

Unfortunate Miss Bailey

A captain bold from Halifax who dwelt in country quarters,
Betrayed a maid who hanged herself one morning in her Garters.
His wicked conscience smited him, he lost his Stomach daily,
And took to drinking Ratafia while thinking of Miss Bailey.

One night betimes he went to bed, for he had caught a Fever;
Says he, "I am a handsome man, but I'm a gay Deceiver."
His candle just at twelve o'clock began to burn quite palely,
A Ghost stepped up to bedside and said "Behold Miss Bailey!"

"Avaunt, Miss Bailey!" then he cried, "Your Face looks white and mealy."
"Dear Captain Smith," the ghost replied, "you've used me ungenteelly:
The Crowner's Quest goes hard with me because I've acted frailly,
And Parson Biggs won't bury me though I am dead Miss Bailey."

"Dear Corpse!" said he, "since you and I accounts must once for all close,
There really is a one pound note in my regimental Smallclothes;
I'll bribe the sexton for your grave." The ghost then vanished gaily
Crying, "Bless you, Wicked Captain Smith, Remember poor Miss Bailey."

On a Clergyman's Horse Biting Him

The steed bit his master;
How came this to pass?
He heard the good pastor
Cry, "All flesh is grass."

She Was Poor but She Was Honest

She was poor, but she was honest,
  Victim of the squire's whim:
First he loved her, then he left her,
  And she lost her honest name.

Then she ran away to London,
  For to hide her grief and shame;
There she met another squire,
  And she lost her name again.

See her riding in her carriage,
  In the Park and all so gay:
All the nibs and nobby persons
  Come to pass the time of day.

See the little old-world village
  Where her aged parents live,
Drinking the champagne she sends them;
  But they never can forgive.

In the rich man's arms she flutters,
  Like a bird with broken wing:
First he loved her, then he left her,
  And she hasn't got a ring.

See him in the splendid mansion,
  Entertaining with the best,
While the girl that he has ruined,
  Entertains a sordid guest.

See him in the House of Commons,
  Making laws to put down crime,
While the victim of his passions
  Trails her way through mud and slime.

Standing on the bridge at midnight,
  She says: "Farewell, blighted Love."
There's a scream, a splash—Good Heavens!
  What is she a-doing of?

Then they dragged her from the river,
  Water from her clothes they wrang,
For they thought that she was drownded;
  But the corpse got up and sang:

"It's the sime the whole world over,
  It's the poor what gets the blime,
It's the rich what gets the pleasure.
  Ain't it all a blooming shime?"

A Strike among the Poets

In his chamber, weak and dying,
  While the Norman baron lay,
Loud, without, his men were crying,
  "Shorter hours and better pay."

Know you why, the ploughman, fretting,
  Homeward plods his weary way
Ere his time? He's after getting
  Shorter hours and better pay.

See! the *Hesperus* is swinging
  Idle in the wintry bay,
And the skipper's daughter's singing,
  "Shorter hours and better pay."

Where's the minstrel boy? I've found him
  Joining in the labour fray
With his placards slung around him.
  "Shorter hours and better pay."

Oh, young Lochinvar is coming;
  Though his hair is getting gray,
Yet I'm glad to hear him humming,
  "Shorter hours and better pay."

E'en the boy upon the burning
  Deck has got a word to say,
Something rather cross concerning
  Shorter hours and better pay.

Lives of great men all remind us
  We can make as much as they,
Work no more, until they find us
  Shorter hours and better pay.

Hail to thee, blithe spirit! (Shelley)
  Wilt thou be a blackleg? Nay.
Soaring, sing above the mêlée,
  "Shorter hours and better pay."

As I Was Laying on the Green

As I was laying on the green,
A small English book I seen.
Carlyle's *Essay on Burns* was the edition,
So I left it laying in the same position.

Lines by an Old Fogy

I'm thankful that the sun and moon
  Are both hung up so high,
That no presumptuous hand can stretch
  And pull them from the sky.

If they were not, I have no doubt
  But some reforming ass
Would recommend to take them down
  And light the world with gas.

Swell's Soliloquy

I don't appwove this hawid waw;
  Those dweadful bannahs hawt my eyes;
And guns and dwums are such a baw—
  Why don't the pawties compwamise?

Of cawce, the toilet has its chawms;
  But why must all the vulgah cwowd
Pawsist in spawting unifawms,
  In cullahs so extwemely loud?

And then the ladies, pwecious deahs!—
  I mawk the change on ev'wy bwow;
Bai Jove! I weally have my feahs
  They wathah like the hawid wow!

To heah the chawming cweatures talk,
  Like patwons of the bloody wing,
Of waw and all its dawty wawk—
  It doesn't seem a pwappah thing!

I called at Mrs. Gweene's last night,
To see her niece, Miss Mawy Hertz,
And found her making—cwushing sight!—
The weddest kind of flannel shirts!

Of cawce, I wose, and sought the daw,
With fawyah flashing fwom my eyes!
I can't appwove this hawid waw—
Why don't the pawties compwamise?

On Thomas Moore's Poems

Lalla Rookh
Is a naughty book
By Tommy Moore,
Who has written four;
Each warmer
Than the former,
So the most recent
Is the least decent.

Belagcholly Days

Chilly Dovebber with his boadigg blast
Dow cubs add strips the beddow add the lawd,
Eved October's suddy days are past—
Add Subber's gawd!

I kdow dot what it is to which I cligg
That stirs to sogg add sorrow, yet I trust
That still I sigg, but as the liddets sigg—
Because I bust.

Add dow, farewell to roses add to birds,
To larded fields and tigkligg streablets eke;
Farewell to all articulated words
I faid would speak.

Farewell, by cherished strolliggs od the sward,
Greed glades add forest shades, farewell to you;
With sorrowing heart I, wretched add forlord,
Bid you—achew!!!

GLOOM

I have a daughter who says the only purpose of a hat is to flirt under. Mr. Anonymous, who shared her cavalier attitude toward prepositions (not propositions) at the end of sentences, said God created tragedy so we'd have something to laugh at. The poems that follow are either very, very gloomy or very, very funny. It's all in the eye of the beholder.

Disgusting

At the boarding house where I live
Things are getting very old.
Long gray hairs in the butter,
And the cheese is green with mold,
When the dog died we had sausage,
When the cat died catnip tea.
When the landlord died I left it;
Spareribs are too much for me.

Rainy days will surely come;
Take your friend's umbrella home.

Somebody Said That It Couldn't Be Done

Somebody said that it couldn't be done—
But he, with a grin, replied
He'd never be one to say it couldn't be done—
Leastways, not till he tried.

So he buckled right in, with a trace of a grin;
By golly, he went right to it.
He tackled The Thing That Couldn't Be Done!
And he couldn't do it.

Adolescence

Oh! to be wafted away
From this black aceldama of sorrow,
Where the dust of an earthy to-day
Makes the earth of a dusty to-morrow.

The Optimist

When the world is all against you;
When the race of life is run;
When the skies have turned to gray again—
Just say, "I've had me fun."
When the friends of yore all turn away
And sadness is the rule,
Just say, "The skies will turn again"
You silly, bloody fool!

The Pessimist

Nothing to do but work!
Nothing! alas, alack!
Nowhere to go but out!
Nowhere to come but back!

My granddad, viewing earth's worn cogs,
Said things were going to the dogs;
His granddad in his house of logs,
Said things were going to the dogs;

His granddad in the Flemish bogs
Said things were going to the dogs;
His granddad in his old skin togs,
Said things were going to the dogs;
There's one thing that I have to state—
The dogs have had a good long wait.

The Old Man

It was a cold and wintry night,
A man stood in the street;
His aged eyes were full of tears,
His boots were full of feet.

LIMERICKS

Though Mr. Anonymous has been associated with innumerable limericks, so far my count of those authentically attributable to him amounts to only one hundred and thirty-three. He deeply resented having his name attached to inferior specimens of the genre, and wrote indignant letters of protest to the editors; but these were never published. One of his limericks summarizes his objection to the common abuses of the form:

The limerick packs laughs anatomical
Into space that is quite economical.
  But the good ones I've seen
  So seldom are clean
And the clean ones so seldom are comical.

His own limericks were always comical, though often a trifle soiled:

There once was a sculptor named Phidias
Whose manners in art were invidious:
  He carved Aphrodite
  Without any nightie,
Which startled the ultrafastidious.

And again:

For the tenth time, dull Daphnis, said Chloe,
You have told me my bosom is snowy;
  You've made much verse on
  Each part of my person—
Now *do* something—there's a good boy!

Mr. Anonymous wrote the limerick of which he was proudest in response to one by Monsignor Ronald Knox, who attended Balliol College at Oxford in the early part of this century. Knox had written:

There once was a man who said: "God
Must think it exceedingly odd
    If he finds that this tree
    Continues to be
When there's no one about in the quad."

To this Berkeleyan concept Uncle Allie replied:

"Dear Sir, Your astonishment's odd;
I am always about in the Quad;
    And that's why the tree
    Will continue to be
Since observed by Yours faithfully, God."

The three limericks that follow are also by Mr. Anonymous. For further examples, you will have to await the publication of my *Encyclopedia Anonymica*.

There was a young lady from Wantage
Of whom the town clerk took advantage.
    Said the borough surveyor:
    'Indeed you must pay 'er.
You've totally altered her frontage.'

There's a wonderful family, called Stein,
There's Gert and there's Epp and there's Ein;
    Gert's poems are bunk,
    Epp's statues are junk,
And no one can understand Ein.

There was an old lady of Ryde
Who ate some green apples, and died.
  The apples (fermented
  Inside the lamented)
Made cider inside 'er inside.

ON LOVE AND RELATED MATTERS

Uncle Allie wrote some moving love poems. The trouble with them, for me, is that they seem so—well—uncharacteristic. I can imagine him weeping in his beer over a dying maiden, but I cannot imagine his weeping without the beer to weep in.

Love Knot

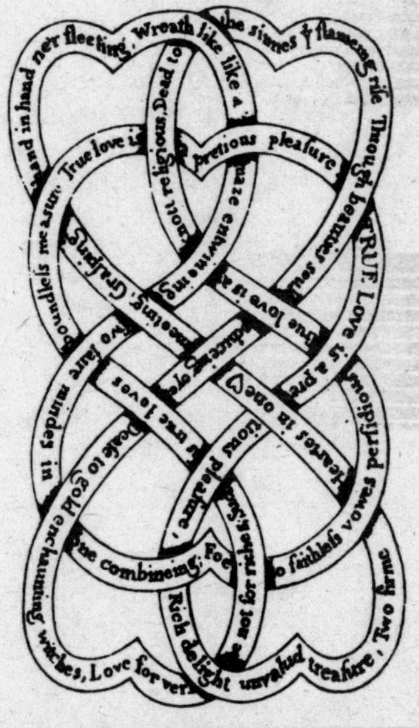

Here's to lying lips,
Though lying lips are bores,
But lying lips are mighty sweet
When they lie next to yours!

❧

Sexually, he was perhaps at his most vulgar in this immortal couplet, written during his stay in London:

Hurray! hurray! The first of May!
Hedgerow fucking begins today!

Minguillo's Kiss

Since for kissing thee, Minguillo,
  Mother's ever scolding me,
Give me swiftly back, thou dear one,
  Give the kiss I gave to thee.
Give me back the kiss—that one, now;
  Let my mother scold no more;
  Let us tell her all is o'er:
What was done is all undone now.
Yes, it will be wise, Minguillo.
  My fond kiss to give to me;
Give me swiftly back, thou dear one
  Give the kiss I gave to thee.
Give me back the kiss, for mother
  Is impatient—prithee, do!
  For that one thou shalt have two:
Give me that, and take another,
Yes, then will they be contented,
  Then can't they complain of me;
Give me swiftly back, thou dear one
  Give the kiss I gave to thee.

Repercussion

They were sitting side by side—
And he sighed, and she sighed.
Said he, "My darling idol"—
And he idled, and she idled.
Said he, "Your hand I asked, so bold I've grown"—
And he groaned, and she groaned.
Said he, "You're cautious, Belle"—
And he bellowed, and she bellowed.

Said he, "You shall have your private gig"—
And he giggled, and she giggled.
Said she, "My dearest Luke"—
And he looked, and she looked.
Said he, "Upon my heart there's such a weight"—
And he waited, and she waited.
Said he, "I'll have thee if thou wilt"—
And he wilted, and she wilted.

Thy heart is like some icy lake,
  On whose cold brink I stand;
  Oh, buckle on my spirit's skate,
And lead, thou living saint, the way
  To where the heart is thin—
That it may break beneath my feet
  And let a lover in!

There Is a Lady Sweet and Kind

There is a lady sweet and kind,
Was never face so pleased my mind,
I did but see her passing by,
And yet I'll love her till I die.

Sabina

Sabina has a thousand charms
  To captivate my heart;
Her lovely eyes are Cupid's arms,
  And every look a dart;
But when the beauteous idiot speaks,
  She cures me of my pain;
Her tongue the servile fetters breaks
  And frees her slave again.

Mr. Anonymous had a protective feeling for young maidens not yet wakened by love, but beginning to stir under the sheets. After a visit to Cheltenham College, a Victorian Seminary for Young Ladies, he summarized as follows the attitude of the students toward their two headmistresses:

Miss Buss and Miss Beale
Cupid's darts do not feel;
Oh, how different from us
Are Miss Beale and Miss Buss.

In a similar vein is this verse written by some Mr. Anonymous of long ago—not exactly a love poem, but close enough:

Prayer to St. Catherine, Patron Saint of Spinsters

St. Catherine, St. Catherine, O lend me thine aid,
And grant that I never may die an old maid.

A husband, St. Catherine,
A *good* one, St. Catherine;
But arn-a-one better than
Narn-a-one, St. Catherine.

Sweet St. Catherine,
A husband, St. Catherine,
Rich, St. Catherine,
Soon, St. Catherine.

False Luve, and Hae Ye Played Me This?

False luve, and hae ye played me this,
In the simmer, mid the flowers?
I sall repay ye back agen
In the winter mid the showers.

But again, dear luve, and again, dear luve,
Will ye not turn again?
As ye look to ither women,
Sall I to ither men.

The Ploughman's Wooing

Quoth John to Joan, wilt thou have me?
I Prithee now wilt, and Ise marry with thee;
My Cow, my Cow, my House and Rents,
And all my Lands and Tenements:
Say *my* Joan, *say my* Joaney, will that not do?
I cannot, cannot, come every day to woe.

I have Corn and Hay in the Barn hard by,
And three fat Hogs pend up in the sty;
I have a Mare and she's coal black;
I ride on her tail to save her back:
Say *my* Joan, *say my* Joaney, will that not do?
I cannot, cannot, come every day to woe.

I have a Cheese upon the shelf,
I cannot eat it all myself;
I have three good Marks that lie in a rag,
In the nook the Chimney instead of a bag:
Say *my* Joan, *say my* Joaney, will that not do?
I cannot, cannot, come every day to woe.

To marry I would have thy consent,
But faith I never could Complement;
I can say nought but hoy gee ho,
Terms that belong to Cart and Plough.
Say *my* Joan, *say my* Joaney, will that not do?
I cannot, cannot, come every day to woe.

Robert Skelton translated this love poem by one of Mr. Anonymous's ancient Greek antecedents:

I Fell in Love. I Kissed.

I fell in love. I kissed. And she
Required no compelling.
But who am I? And who is she?
I tell you, I'm not telling.

⁂

Some of the more serious verses were surely written by earlier incarnations of Mr. Anonymous. The two that follow, though, bear the unmistakable stamp of Uncle Allie:

A Toast

Here's to you and here's to me,
And here's to the girl with the well-shaped knee.
Here's to the man with his hand on her garter;
He hasn't got far yet, but he's a damn good starter.

Minnie the Mermaid

Many's the night I spent with Minnie the
  Mermaid,
Down at the bottom of the sea.
She forgot her morals, down among the corals,
Gee but she was mighty good to me.

Many's the night when the pale moon was
  shining,
Down on her bungalow.
Ashes to ashes, dust to dust,
Two twin beds and only one of them mussed.

Oh it's easy to see she's not my mother,
'Cause my mother's forty-nine.
And it's easy to see she's not my sister,
'Cause I'd never give my sister such a helluva
  good time.

And it's easy to see she's not my sweetie,
'Cause my sweetie's too refined.
She's just a cute little kid who never knew what
  she did,
She's just a personal friend of mine.

I suspect that *Minnie the Mermaid* is really two or more poems that got together by mistake, but I present it as I found it in Uncle Allie's papers.

ON MARRIAGE

Uncle Allie paid moving tribute to married love. Generally, though, he preferred to make fun of it. Like the fox that lost its brush and urged all the other foxes to cut off theirs, he had no choice but to pretend that his miserable bachelor state was Paradise epitomized. He admitted, ever so slightly shamefaced, responsibility for a quatrain that children were already chanting long before I was born:

Hogamous higamous
Men are polygamous
Higamous hogamous
Women monogamous.

Wine, Women and Wedding

The glances over cocktails
That seemed to be so sweet
Don't seem quite so amorous
Over the Shredded Wheat.

The Bad-Tempered Wife

A farmer was plowing in his field one day,
When the devil came and to him did say,
"See here, my good man, I have come for your wife,
For she's the bane and torment of your life."

So the devil he h'isted her upon his back,
And down to hell with her he did pack;
But when they got there the gates they were shut,
With a sweep of her arm she laid open his nut.

There stood a small devil with ball and with chains,
She upped with her foot and she kicked out his brains;

Six little devils jumped over the wall,
Saying, "Take her back, daddy, she'll murder us all."

So the devil he h'isted her upon his back,
And up to the earth with her he did pack;
"See here, my good man, I've come with your wife,
For she's the bane and torment of my life."

The devil he said to the farmer then,
"You keep her; I don't want to see her again.
From the look on her face everybody can tell
She's not fit for heaven and she's too mean for hell."

What did I get married for?
　That's what I want to know:
I was led to the altar
　Like a lamb to the slaughter.
We met on a Friday;
　My luck was out, I'm sure:
I took her for better or worse, but she
　Was worse than I took her for.

Panegyric on the Ladies
(READ ALTERNATE LINES)

That man must lead a happy life
　Who's free from matrimonial chains,
Who is directed by a wife
　Is sure to suffer for his pains.

Adam could find no solid peace
　When Eve was given for a mate;
Until he saw a woman's face
　Adam was in a happy state.

In all the female race appear
　Hypocrisy, deceit, and pride;
Truth, darling of a heart sincere,
　In woman never did reside.

What tongue is able to unfold
  The failings that in woman dwell?
The worth in woman we behold
  Is almost imperceptible.

Confusion take the man, I say,
  Who changes from his singleness,
Who will not yield to woman's sway
  Is sure of earthly blessedness.

The Devonshire Lane

In a Devonshire lane, as I trotted along,
T'other day much in want of a subject for song,
Thinks I to myself, I have hit on a strain,—
Sure marriage is much like a Devonshire lane.

In the first place, 'tis long, and when once you are in it,
It holds you as fast as the cage holds a linnet;
For howe'er rough and dirty the road may be found,
Drive forward you must, since there's no turning round.

MISCELLANY

Most of Mr. Anonymous's verses were not aimed at any particular target; they just happened. Here is a clutch of idle conceits, including a verse made up of lines from other poets, a sort of nursery rhyme, a countryman's superstition, and a punctuation puzzle.

Life

1. Why all this toil for triumphs of an hour?
2. Life's a short summer, man a flower.
3. By turns we catch the vital breath and die—
4. The cradle and the tomb, alas! so nigh.
5. To be, is better far than not to be.
6. Though all man's life may seem a tragedy;
7. But light cares speak when mighty griefs are dumb,
8. The bottom is but shallow whence they come.
9. Your fate is but the common lot of all:
10. Unmingled joys here to no man befall,
11. Nature to each allots his proper sphere;
12. Fortune makes folly her peculiar care;
13. Custom does often reason overrule,
14. And throw a cruel sunshine on a fool.
15. Live well; how long or short, permit to Heaven;
16. They who forgive most, shall be most forgiven.
17. Sin may be clasped so close we cannot see its face—
18. Vile intercourse where virtue has no place.
19. Then keep each passion down, however dear;
20. Thou pendulum betwixt a smile and tear.
21. Her sensual snares, let faithless pleasure lay,
22. With craft and skill, to ruin and betray;
23. Soar not too high to fall, but stoop to rise.

24. We masters grow of all that we despise.
25. Oh, then, renounce that impious self-esteem;
26. Riches have wings, and grandeur is a dream.
27. Think not ambition wise because 'tis brave,
28. The paths of glory lead but to the grave.
29. What is ambition?—'tis a glorious cheat!—
30. Only destructive to the brave and great.
31. What's all the gaudy glitter of a crown?
32. The way to bliss lies not on beds of down.
33. How long we live, not years but actions tell;
34. That man lives twice who lives the first life well.
35. Make, then, while yet ye may, your God your friend,
36. Whom Christians worship yet not comprehend.
37. The trust that's given guard, and to yourself be just;
38. For, live how we can, yet die we must.

1. Young; 2. Dr. Johnson; 3. Pope; 4. Prior; 5. Sewell; 6. Spenser; 7. Daniell; 8. Sir Walter Raleigh; 9. Longfellow; 10. Southwell; 11. Congreve; 12. Churchill; 13. Rochester; 14. Armstrong; 15. Milton; 16. Bailey; 17. Trench; 18. Somerville; 19. Thomson; 20. Byron; 21. Smollet; 22. Crabbe; 23. Massinger; 24. Cowley; 25. Beattie; 26. Cowper; 27. Sir Walter Davenant; 28. Gray; 29. Willis; 30. Addison; 31. Dryden; 32. Francis Quarles; 33. Watkins; 34. Herrick; 35. William Mason; 36. Hill; 37. Dana; 38. Shakespeare.

A Man of Words

A man of words and not of deeds,
Is like a garden full of weeds;
And when the weeds begin to grow,
It's like a garden full of snow;
And when the snow begins to fall,
It's like a bird upon the wall;
And when the bird away does fly,
It's like an eagle in the sky;

❧

And when the sky begins to roar,
It's like a lion at the door;
And when the door begins to brack,
It's like a stick across your back;
And when your back begins to smart,
It's like a penknife in your heart;
And when your heart begins to bleed,
You're dead, and dead, and dead indeed.

Ambiguous Lines
(READ WITH A COMMA AFTER THE FIRST NOUN IN EACH LINE)

I saw a peacock with a fiery tail
I saw a blazing comet pour down hail
I saw a cloud all wrapt with ivy round
I saw a lofty oak creep on the ground
I saw a beetle swallow up a whale
I saw a foaming sea brimful of ale
I saw a pewter cup sixteen feet deep
I saw a well full of men's tears that weep
I saw wet eyes in flames of living fire
I saw a house as high as the moon and higher
I saw the glorious sun at deep midnight
I saw the man who saw this wondrous sight.
I saw a pack of cards gnawing a bone
I saw a dog seated on Britain's throne
I saw King George shut up within a box
I saw an orange driving a fat ox
I saw a butcher not a twelvemonth old
I saw a great-coat all of solid gold
I saw two buttons telling of their dreams
I saw my friends who wished I'd quit these themes.

NONSENSE

Nonsense, said Mr. Anonymous, is the mother of wisdom; he did not say who the father was. Some of the most provocative lines in Shakespeare are uttered by the kings' fools.

Mr. Anonymous wrote nonsense by the ream. I have to confess, though, that I have found little wisdom in it.

Whenceness of the Which
(SOME DISTANCE AFTER TENNYSON)

Come into the Whenceness Which,
  For the fierce Because has flown:
Come into the Whenceness Which,
  I am here by the where alone;
And the Whereas odors are wafted abroad
  Till I hold my nose and groan.

Queen Which of the Whichbud garden of What's
  Come hither the jig is done.
In gloss of Isness and shimmer of Was,
  Queen Thisness and which in one;
Sing out, little Which, sunning over the bangs,
  To the Nowness, and be it sun.

There has fallen a splendid tear
  From the Is flower at the fence;
She is coming, my Which, my dear,
  And as she Whistles a song of the Whence,
The Nowness cries, "She is near, she is near."
  And the Thingness howls, "Alas!"
The Whoness murmurs, "Well, I should smile,"
  And the Whatlet sobs, "I pass."

'Tis Midnight

'Tis midnight, and the setting sun
   Is slowly rising in the west;
The rapid rivers slowly run,
   The frog is on his downy nest.
The pensive goat and sportive cow,
Hilarious, leap from bough to bough.

Sonnet Found in a Deserted Madhouse

Oh that my soul a marrow-bone might seize!
For the old egg of my desire is broken,
Spilled is the pearly white and spilled the yolk, and
As the mild melancholy contents grease
My path the shorn lamb baas like bumblebees.
Time's trashy purse is as a taken token
Or like a thrilling recitation, spoken
By mournful mouths filled full of mirth and cheese.

And yet, why should I clasp the earthful urn?
Or find the frittered fig that felt the fast?
Or choose to chase the cheese around the churn?
Or swallow any pill from out the past?
Ah no, love, not while your hot kisses burn
Like a potato riding on the blast.

I Cannot Wash My Eye without an Eyecup

I cannot wash my eye without an eyecup,
To find this out, dear, ten long years it took,
And if it were not for my scruples,
I'd go round with filthy pupils,
Giving everyone I know a dirty look.

The Budding Bronx

Der spring is sprung
Der grass is riz
I wonder where dem boidies is?

Der little boids is on der wing,
Ain't dat absoid?
Der little wings is on der boid!

An Accident Happened

An accident happened to my brother Jim
When somebody threw a tomato at him—
Tomatoes are juicy and don't hurt the skin,
But this one was specially packed in a tin.

Warning to Parents

Three children sliding on the ice
   Upon a summer's day,
   It so fell out they all fell in,
   The rest they ran away.

Now had these children been at home
   Or sliding on dry ground,
Ten thousand pounds to one penny
   They had not all been drown'd.

You parents all that children have,
   And you that eke have none,
If you would have them safe abroad,
   Pray keep them safe at home.

A Love Song by a Lunatic

There's not a spider in the sky,
  There's not a glowworm in the sea,
There's not a crab that soars on high,
  But bids me dream, dear maid, of thee!

When watery Phoebus ploughs the main,
  When fiery Luna gilds the lea,
As flies run up the window-pane,
  So fly my thoughts, dear love, to thee!

PARODIES

Mr. Anonymous was quite a sensible man in most ways, but he could not break himself of the habit of writing parodies. A book has been published of his parodies on Whitman alone. He must have burlesqued Hamlet's Soliloquy two dozen times.

Parodies quickly grow repetitious, and I tire of them easily. If they were not so major a part of Uncle Allie's corpus, I'd be tempted to drop the following examples altogether.

The Bather's Dirge
(AFTER TENNYSON)

Break, break, break,
  On thy cold, hard stones, O sea!
And I hope that my tongue won't utter
  The curses that rise in me.

Oh, well for the fisherman's boy,
  If he likes to be soused with the spray!
Oh, well for the sailor lad,
  As he paddles about in the bay!

And the ships swim happily on,
  To their haven under the hill;
But O for a clutch of that vanished hand,
  And a kick—for I'm catching a chill!

Break, break, break,
  At my poor bare feet, O sea!
But the artful scamp who has collar'd my clothes
  Will never come back to me.

Nursery Rhymes a la Mode
(AFTER OSCAR WILDE)

(Our nurseries will soon be too cultured to admit the old rhymes in their philistine and unaesthetic garb. They may be redressed somewhat on this model.)

Oh, but she was dark and shrill,
(Hey-de-diddle and hey-de-dee!)
The cat that (on the first April)
Played the fiddle on the lea.
Oh, and the moon was wan and bright,
(Hey-de-diddle and hey-de-dee!)
The Cow she looked nor left nor right,
But took it straight at a jump, pardie!
The hound did laugh to see this thing,
(Hey-de-diddle and hey-de-dee!)
As it was parlous wantoning,
(Ah, good my gentles, laugh not ye,)
And underneath a dreesome moon
Two lovers fled right piteouslie;
A spooney plate with a plated spoon,
(Hey-de-diddle and hey-de-dee!)

Postscript:

Then blame me not, altho' my verse
  Sounds like an echo of C.S.C.
Since still they make ballads that worse and worse
  Savor of diddle and hey-de-dee.

The Amateur Flute
(AFTER POE)

Hear the fluter with his flute,
    Silver flute!
Oh, what a world of wailing is awakened by its toot!
  How it demi-semi quavers
    In the maddened air of night!
  And defieth all endeavors
    To escape the sound or sigh

Of the flute, flute, flute,
With its tootle, tootle, toot;
With reiterated tootling of exasperating toots,
The long protracted tootlings of agonizing toots
Of the flute, flute, flute,
Flute, flute, flute,
And the wheezings and the spittings of its toots.
Should he get that other flute
Golden flute,
Oh, what a deeper anguish will his presence institoot!
How his eyes to heaven he'll raise,
As he plays
All the days!
How he'll stop us on our ways
With its praise!
And the people—oh, the people,
That don't live up in the steeple
But inhabit Christian parlors
Where he visiteth and plays,
Where he plays, plays, plays
In the cruellest of ways,
And thinks we ought to listen,
And expects us to be mute,
Who would rather have the earache
Than the music of his flute,
Of his flute, flute, flute,
And the tootings of his toot,
Of the toots wherewith he tootleth its agonizing toot,
Of the flute, flewt, fluit, floot,
Phlute, phlewt, phlewght,
And the tootle, tootle, tooting of its toot.

(AFTER LONGFELLOW)

Under a spreading gooseberry bush the village burglar lies,
The burglar is a hairy man with whiskers round his eyes,

And the muscles of his brawny arms keep off the little flies.

He goes on Sunday to the church to hear the Parson shout.
He puts a penny in the plate and takes a pound note out,
And drops a conscience-stricken tear in case he is found out.

Justice to Scotland
(AFTER BURNS)

O mickle yeuks the keckle doup,
An' a' unsicker girns the graith,
For wae and wae! the crowdies loup
O'er jouk an' hallan, braw an' baith.
Where ance the coggie hirpled fair,
And blithesome poortith toomed the loof,
There's nae a burnie giglet rare
But blaws in ilka jinking coof.

The routhie bield that gars the gear
Is gone where glint the pawky een,
And aye the stound is birkin lear
Where sconnered yowies wheeped yestreen,
The creeshie rax wi' skelpin' kaes
Nae mair the howdie bicker whangs,
Nor weanies in their wee bit claes
Glour light as lamies wi' their sangs.

Yet leeze me on my bonnie byke!
My drappie aiblins blinks the noo,
An' leesome luve has lapt the dyke
Forgatherin' just a wee bit fou.
And Scotia! while thy rantin' lunt
Is mirk and moop with gowans fine,
I'll stowling pit my unco brunt,
An' cleek my duds for auld lang syne.

Toothache
(AFTER SHAKESPEARE)

To have it out or not. That is the question—
Whether 'tis better for the jaws to suffer
The pangs and torments of an aching tooth,
Or to take steel against a host of troubles,
And, by extracting, end them. To pull—to tug!—
No more: and by a tug to say we end
The toothache and a thousand natural ills
The jaw is heir to. 'Tis a consummation
Devoutly to be wished! To pull—to tug!—
To tug—perchance to break! Ay, there's the rub,
For in that wrench what agonies may come
When we have half dislodged the stubborn foe,
Must give us pause. There's the respect
That makes an aching tooth of so long life.
For who would bear the whips and stings of pain,
The old wife's nostrum, dentist's contumely;
The pangs of hope deferred, kind sleep's delay;
The insolence of pity, and the spurns,
That patient sickness of the healthy takes,
When he himself might his quietus make
For one poor shilling? Who would fardels bear,
To groan and sink beneath a load of pain,
But that the dread of something lodged within
The linen-twisted forceps, from whose pangs
No jaw at ease returns, puzzles the will,
And makes it rather bear those ills it has
Than fly to others that it knows not of?
Thus dentists do make cowards of us all,
And thus the native hue of resolution
Is sicklied o'er with the pale cast of fear;
And many a one, whose courage seeks the door,
With this regard his footsteps turns away,
Scared at the name of dentist.

A LAST WORD

I have been unfair to Mr. Anonymous in this book. I have slighted his more serious work, partly because I lack the agility to leap back and forth like a mountain goat between grave and gay, and partly because I did not want the book to wobble too much on its bottom.

But Mr. Anonymous was at times a fine poet. You will seldom read lovelier or sadder lines than these, written, in imitation of an earlier style, while he was studying at Edinburgh University in the 1890s.

The Falcon

I
Lully, lulley! lully, lulley!
The faucon hath born my make away!
II
He bare him up, he bare him down,
He bare him into an orchard brown.
III
In that orchard was an hall,
That was hanged with purple and pall.
IV
And in that hall there was a bed,
It was hangèd with gold sa red.
V
And in that bed there li'th a knight,
His woundès bleeding day and night.
VI
At the bed's foot there li'th a hound,
Licking the blood as it runs down.
VII
By that bed-side kneeleth a may,
As she weepeth both night and day.

VIII

And at the bed's head standeth a stone,
Corpus Christi written thereon.

IX

Lully, lulley! lully, lulley!
The faucon hath born my make away.

INDEX OF FIRST LINES

❧§❧

About the Author

Willard R. Espy is the author of *The Game of Words, An Almanac of Words at Play*, and *Oysterville*. Born in Oysterville, Washington, he has spent most of his life in New York City, where his long literary career has included such varied positions as reporter, correspondent, editor, promotion chief, and writer. His light verse and articles have appeared in *The Nation, The Atlantic, Harper's, The New York Times Magazine, Harvard Magazine, American Heritage, Reader's Digest, Punch*, and other magazines.